YULETIDE PUNCH

PHANTOM QUEEN DIARIES BOOK 12

SHAYNE SILVERS
CAMERON O'CONNELL

ARGENTO
PUBLISHING

CONTENTS

Shayne Silvers & Cameron O'Connell

Yuletide Punch

The Phantom Queen Diaries Book 12

A TempleVerse Series

ISBN 13: 978-1-947709-84-3

© 2021, Shayne Silvers / Argento Publishing, LLC

info@shaynesilvers.com

SHAYNE AND CAMERON

Shayne Silvers, here.

Cameron O'Connell is one helluva writer, and he's worked tire-lessly to merge a story into the Temple Verse that would provide a different and unique *voice*, but a complementary *tone* to my other novels. SOME people might say I'm hard to work with. But certainly, Cameron would never...

Hey! Pipe down over there, author monkey! Get back to your writing cave and finish the next Phantom Queen Novel!

Ahem. Now, where was I?

This is book 12 in the Phantom Queen Diaries, which is a series that ties into the existing TempleVerse with Nate Temple and Callie Penrose. This series could also be read independently if one so chose. Then again, you, the reader, will get SO much more out of my existing books (and this series) by reading them all in tandem.

But that's not up to us. It's up to you, the reader.

You tell us...

CHAPTER 1

The world as I knew it pitched violently as I was unceremoniously flipped upside down—a vertigo made that much worse by the copious amounts of alcohol sloshing around in my otherwise empty stomach. The men who'd done the deed, a leering pair smelling of stale beer and honeyed mead, held me up by my thighs. I couldn't tell you their names; I hadn't asked, and they hadn't offered.

But then I think we all knew what they wanted from a good little reformed Catholic schoolgirl like me.

"Don't ye lads get any funny ideas, now," I warned in a slightly slurred voice. "If ye like your eyes where they are, I suggest ye keep 'em to yourselves."

"What'd she say?" asked the fairer of the two companions.

"Something about licking our eyes, I think."

"Is that some kind of new fetish? Because I don't think I'd be into that."

"That's what you said about the pinky finger thing."

"Hey, I told you that in confidence!"

"Oy! I said *like*," I corrected them, loudly. "*Like* your eyes."

"Oh, well that's nice of you to say."

"We like yours, too," the other added.

"No, I—nevermind. Shut up so I can concentrate." I paused to take a long breath. It was harder to think straight with all that blood rushing to my head. So tough, in fact, that I had to talk myself through the steps just to be sure I hadn't skipped anything. "So, I'm upside down. That's done. I've already got hold of the keg. Or, ye know, the cask or whatever. This t'ing."

I slapped the side of the wooden barrel that had inspired this half-cocked idea in the first place, then planted both hands on its lip and used it to steady myself once more.

"How long are we supposed to keep holding her up like this?" said one of my spotters to the other in a voice too loud to be considered a whisper.

"How should I know? You're the one who got all cow-eyed and said we should listen to her."

"Like you were going to tell her no! Besides, how was I supposed to know she'd be so much heavier than she looks?"

I reached out to swat at the one who'd made that comment but missed. "Hey! What did I just say about shutting up?! Now I'll have to go over it again."

"Sorry!"

"We'll be quiet."

I grunted an acknowledgement. "That's better."

In most places, a stunt like this might have attracted some unwanted attention, but I doubted anyone here would even notice, let alone care. It was already pretty late, which meant the evening feast had already been served and consumed, the skalds were playing crowd favorites, the lovers were busy romping on their bearskin rugs, and the fighters were, well, fighting. Indeed, I could hear raised voices and the clash of swords nearby.

Distracted by the noise, I craned my neck in search of the participants on the off chance I recognized them, but was instead greeted by a veritable curtain of ginger locks obscuring my already impaired vision. Annoyed, I tried to fling my hair to one side, but it seemed the mane had grown far too long and unruly for that.

"Uh oh, looks like I'm seein' red," I muttered, then giggled to myself. "Hair's so stupid."

"Is she talking to herself?"

"If she is, it's your fault. You always get us mixed up with the hot, crazy ones."

"I do not!"

"What about Tammy? Remember her?"

"Oh come on. How was I supposed to know where she got all those tongues?"

"Fine. Kimbra."

"I thought she was into me!"

"She wanted to sacrifice you to the Allfather for a new pair of shoes!"

"In all fairness, they *were* a very nice pair of shoes. You don't see that sort of quality leatherwork these days."

"Oy! Ye do realize I can hear the two of ye, right?!" I snapped. "Stop all your chatter and let me focus, already. I'm tryin' to remember what comes next."

"Uh oh, she's getting mad."

"What a Kimbra."

"Got it!" I shouted, interrupting them before they could begin yet another inane conversation. I rapped my knuckles against the lid of the barrel and pointed to my mouth. "I need to get what's in here in *here*."

"How?"

I tried to shrug but, braced as I was between them and the cask, managed only the awkward wiggle of a twitching fish instead. I coughed to hide my embarrassment. "Ahem. Well, to tell ye the truth, I was never in charge of that part. Plus it's been a while. The last time I tried somethin' like this I was crashin' a really weird Harvard party thrown by a sorority full of succubi. Long story. Anyway, I'm pretty sure some sort of hose is involved. And a pump. There was definitely a pump."

My spotters exchanged looks of confusion.

I sighed, realizing far too late the rather glaring tactical error I'd made. "Ye don't have anything' like that here, do ye?"

Both men shrugged simultaneously, causing me to bob awkwardly up and down in a way that made me want to lose my lunch. I took a moment to quell that urge before shaking my head in regret.

"Of course ye don't. Guess this means no cask stands for us, after all. Ye might as well put me down."

They did as I suggested, their faces flushed with drink and the exertion of holding up a woman damn near as tall as they were— albeit considerably less muscular. But then, how was I supposed to compete with a pair of brawny, long-legged sea raiders from a bygone era whose idea of accessorizing was braiding knuckle bones into each other's beards?

"Oy," I said, turning to the two men and squinting. "What're your names, anyway? Ye never said."

"I'm Dolph," said the dark-haired one. "And this is my brother, Lundgren."

"Dolph...Lundgren," I replied, my gaze oscillating back and forth between the pair. "Your names are Dolph and Lundgren?"

They nodded in unison.

"And what about you?" Lundgren asked. "What's your name?"

"Stella," I lied. "Stella Own. But ye can call me the Italian Stallion. No, no, wait. Wait. The Irish...oh, shite. What rhymes with Irish?"

Dolph leaned in and whispered to his brother. "Total Tammy."

Lundgren nodded, gravely.

"Forget it," I said with a sigh. "Ye can just call me Quinn."

"Quinn?" Dolph echoed. "That's an unusual name."

"Like ye two can talk," I muttered, rolling my eyes. "Dolph freakin' Lundgren. Give us a break."

"Huh?"

"Nevermind. Ye wouldn't understand."

Dolph smiled nervously. "Alright, well, if that's all we really should be getting back. We have..."

"Friends," Lungren added, helpfully. "Friends who are expecting us. Sorry. We'd love to stick around, it's just...well, you know how it is."

I frowned as I realized the two of them were making excuses to get away from me. I supposed it should've hurt, but I didn't necessarily blame them; I was a stranger. More than that, I was *strange*. I didn't belong here, and we all knew it. But you know what they say...

When in Valhalla, do as the Valhallans do.

Or was it what happens in Valhalla stays in Valhalla?

Either way, I could use another drink.

"Wait!" I exclaimed, suddenly. "What about a beer bong?!"

Dolph hesitated. "A beer bong?"

"Aye, it's like this funnel t'ing ye pour beer into while the other person gets down on one knee and drinks as much as they can as fast as they can. They do it all the time in Midgard."

"In Midgard?!" Lundgren grabbed his brother's arm. "Dolph! We have to try it!"

Dolph, however, seemed far less enthused. "No offense, but how do we know this won't be a colossal waste of time?"

"Ye don't," I admitted. "But this will be a lot easier, I swear. All we need is a really big drinkin' horn. Or a super long one. Whichever. It should work, either way."

I was nearly out of breath by the time I finished, aware I sounded far more desperate than I'd have liked. But then, my buzz was fading far too fast for my liking, and with soberness came feelings I could neither place nor comprehend. Feelings of guilt and shame. Indeed, if I'd learned anything since arriving here it was that I vastly preferred the comfortably numb sensation, and that I was already starting to run low on anesthesia.

Lundgren leaned over and whispered conspiratorially in his brother's ear. "Do you think she's talking about *the* Drinking Horn?"

"What?" Dolph glanced at his brother in confusion that soon turned into revulsion. "Of course not! No one's crazy enough to drink from that thing. Not even Kimbra."

"I mean, I wouldn't underestimate Kimbra," Lungren replied,

sagely. "She's from the South. They do things with alcohol that...just aren't right."

"What is with ye two and talkin' about me like I'm not here?" I demanded, jabbing both men in their beefy chests before they could go on with their senseless diatribe. "Ye better knock it off, or I'll make ye regret it!"

"Regret it, how?" Lundgren asked, his eyes wide.

I frowned, scouring my memories for an appropriate punishment. "I'll...I'll draw tiny penises all over your faces while you're sleepin'. In permanent ink."

"You wouldn't!"

"She's obviously joking, brother," Dolph interjected.

"I never joke about penises." I hesitated, then held up a finger. "Actually, I take that back. I *occasionally* joke about penises. But no, seriously. I'll draw a dick on your face."

Dolph turned to me, startled.

"What?" I said, combatively. "Listen, I don't make the rules."

"Rules?"

"Sure. Ye know, like whoever smelt it dealt it. Or she who strikes first wins. That sort of t'ing."

The brothers stared at me with strikingly similar, equally baffled expressions.

I waved that away. "Forget it. All I'm sayin' is that, when it comes to idle threats, I'm all about follow-through. I've shot like seven people for movin' after I told 'em not to. And that was for, like, fidgetin'."

Dolph anxiously cleared his throat. "Please allow us to apologize."

"We're very sorry," Lundgren added, hanging his head. "And it won't happen again. We promise. Just don't draw genitalia on our faces. Please."

"Don't worry." I patted both their arms reassuringly. "I accept your apologies."

The brothers exchanged looks of relief.

"But if ye *really* wanted to make it up to me," I continued, slinging my arms over both their shoulders and dragging my new chums away from the forgotten cask and farther into the enormous mead hall they called home, "you'll take me to see this so-called Drinkin' Horn."

CHAPTER 2

The Drinking Horn hung horizontally from the rafters, held aloft by absurdly large, gold-plated chains that reflected the lustrous glow of firelight which perpetually lit this otherworldly place. The Horn itself was more impressive still, reminding me of a gigantic dinosaur's tooth I once saw displayed at a science exhibit. Of course, that installation had been a plaster mold painted porcelain white and aggrandized to wow the kids who had to walk beneath it.

This fixture, on the other hand, was very much the real deal: curved like a hollowed out eel with its head cut off, the outer horn appeared as if it had been dipped in tar, its narrow tip as black as its base was white. Moreover, I was pretty sure I could crawl up inside the thing and take a nap if I was so inclined—to give you an idea of just how large it was.

"It originally belonged to the Jötunn," Lundgren said beside me. "The giants."

"Until Thor snuck off with it," Dolph added. "They say he got wasted off his ass and left it here a few nights before, well...you know."

I cocked my head. "Before what?"

The brothers exchanged glances.

"Before he, uh..." Lundgren looked to his brother for help.

"Died," Dolph whispered.

"Oh, right. That."

I nodded along amiably, though frankly I wasn't paying that much attention; I was far more interested in just how much booze was likely to fit in that delightful monstrosity, not to mention the method by which I might get said booze into my mouth. Maybe if I used the chains to tip it over, somehow? Or maybe I could recruit one of those giants they'd mentioned. I seemed to recall knowing one, though her name and face escaped me.

Oh well, it'd come to me. For now, I decided to sneak a closer look. I craned my neck to either side, expecting to find a velvet rope or some such blocking my path.

There wasn't one.

"Hey, what do you think you're—"

"You can't—"

I waved the two einherjar off and clambered up onto the nearest dais to inspect the chains. Despite their complaints, no one else seemed to notice what I was up to, or even care. In fact, the sounds of merrymaking only increased as somewhere behind us a band of drunken louts began singing an oddly familiar, festive tune that was soon taken up by a dozen other tables. I eventually recognized it as a carol of some sort, though not one I'd ever heard.

Ignoring them, I reached up to run a hand along the surface of what must have once belonged to a beast of unimaginable size. The Drinking Horn was smooth to the touch and eerily, almost supernaturally, cold. Like a glass mug left in the freezer.

"The world's greatest beer bong," I whispered to myself. "I've finally found ye."

"Excuse me? What is it you're doing over there?"

Startled by the unexpected question, I yanked my hand back and whipped around like a horny teenager caught fondling something they weren't supposed to. I quickly saw that the voice belonged to a woman—and an armed woman, at that.

The newcomer had white blonde hair and wore it braided tight to her scalp, accentuating the structure of her heart-shaped face. A neat little scar bisected her bottom lip and chin as if she'd slipped and sliced it open as a little girl. Chainmail shimmered beneath her floor-length emerald cloak, its hem and collar trimmed with white fur interwoven with holly and tiny silver bells.

"Who, me?" I asked, feigning innocence. "I was just admirin' this here horn with me friends."

"Oh? And what friends would those be?"

I frowned and glanced back over my shoulder only to see Dolph and Lundgren retreating into a crowd of passionate revelers with their heads down and their eyes averted.

Cowards.

I sighed. "I take it I'm not supposed to touch the merchandise?"

"The what?"

"The Drinkin' Horn."

"Ah. No, though strictly speaking there are no rules against it. It's simply not recommended."

"Why not?"

"Does it matter?" The woman shrugged. "It's not like anyone here could drink from it, even if they wanted to."

"And why's that?"

"Wh—" She cocked an eyebrow at me. "Because it weighs several tons, for one thing. And because the only Aesir who dared to drink from it was Thor. And even *he* risked death in the attempt. That's why."

"Sounds like he'd be a good drinkin' buddy. Shame he wound up dead."

The armed woman frowned, her eyes narrowed as she searched my face—though what she intended to find there I couldn't be sure. "What's your name?"

I considered telling her but decided against it; something about her appearance had triggered a feeling of longing inside me. A sense not unlike encountering a picture of a treasured memory in the back of a drawer long shut.

"What's yours?" I asked, instead.

"I asked you first."

"Guess we're at an impasse, then, aren't we?" I offered her a thin-lipped smile, then reached out to pat the Drinking Horn. "Don't worry, gorgeous, I'll be back for ye. And next time, I'll make sure we're properly acquainted. No interruptions."

"Hold on a moment, are you—"

"Sorry!" I waved off the nosy woman and whatever impertinent question she'd been preparing to ask. "I've got to see a man about an eight-legged horse."

She opened her mouth to say something else, but I'd already left her behind for the crowds gathered round the long tables that occupied the center of the mead hall. I briefly considered searching for the brothers Dolph and Lundgren, but ultimately decided against it; there were plenty of other strapping young Saxons I could rope into shenanigans if the mood struck.

Besides, I had other priorities.

"Here drinky drinky drinky drinky..."

As if on cue, I heard a heavy thunk from just beyond a cluster of bearded einherjar with giggling barmaids straddling their laps. The sound repeated itself, audible above what sounded suspiciously like a death metal rendition of "I Saw Mommy Kissing Santa Claus" in F Minor played by a nearby skald.

Then again.

Assuming the thunks to be the sound of freshly filled flagons being slammed onto an empty bar top, I fought my way past the throngs until I came upon a less congested patch of floor. Sadly, it soon became clear that the noise I'd heard had nothing to do with alcohol and everything to do with axes.

I groaned and plopped down, watching as a half-dozen puffed up, half-naked men with more body hair than sense hoisted throwing axes and chucked them in haphazard intervals at targets painted on the nearest wall. Their audience—made up almost exclusively of other, equally objectionable men—cheered and cajoled in equal measure as the axe blades soared through the air. I glared at them all as they patted each other's backs and clapped mugs, sloshing perfectly good ale all over the floor.

"Idgets," I muttered.

"Well cut off my right hand and call me Tyr! You actually came! Finally realized what you were missing out on, eh? Or did you come to sign up for our Midwinter tournament? You won't believe the prizes we've got this year."

A clipboard was shoved into my hands before I could respond, though I wasn't surprised when I finally caught sight of the potbellied dwarf who'd accosted me. And no, before you say it, I didn't mean a little person. I meant a dwarf—a card-carrying craftsman born from the flesh of a dying god, complete with jutting ears, sable-skin, and shock white hair.

Worse still, it was a dwarf I knew fairly well.

"Hello, Glow. Fancy seein' ye here."

The dwarf made an exasperated sound, though his smile never wavered. "I told you, it's not Glow. It's Glói. But seriously, I'm so pleased you finally decided to take me up on my offer. I'm really hoping to expand our brand. You know, capitalize on the emerging female market."

"Maybe try lettin' 'em throw the axes at the men instead of targets. I'm sure that'd do the trick."

"You know, you're not the first of your kind to suggest that."

"What can I say? We really aren't that complicated when ye get right down to it." I turned my attention to the sheet of parchment pinned to the clipboard in my hand and pointed at the header displayed across the top. "Does this say 'AA'?"

Glow, whose real name I could neither spell nor pronounce, nodded amicably. "That's right. It stands for Axes and Ale, not to be confused with our competitors, Arts and Crafts with Ale."

The dwarf pointed idly towards the far end of the mead hall where I saw an assembly line of einherjar whittling wood, sewing clothes, and sharpening blades. A few hung topless over the back of chairs while others painted intricate tattoos across their flesh, their brows knitted in pain and slick with sweat. I watched as a barmaid came by and replaced their empty mugs.

"And I thought I was hardcore," I muttered.

"Anyway, how about it?" Glow continued, exhibiting the trademark enthusiasm I'd come to know and hate. He thrust one curiously long and articulate finger onto the page and tapped. "Would you like to sign up?"

I was about to decline and return Glow's clipboard when a nearby axe-thrower—this one so big and furry he might very well have been part black bear—strutted over and snatched the clipboard out of my hands.

"No women," he insisted, sneering.

"Why not?" I asked, more curious than offended. Frankly, I'd gotten used to this sort of treatment; toxic masculinity was sort of a theme in a realm designed for combatant drunks.

"Because women miss. Their axes bounce. Everyone knows that."

"And men don't? Miss, I mean."

"Never."

"Then how come ye lot can't seem to manage gettin' it all in the urinal, huh?"

"What?"

"I'm just sayin', if I had an attachment that pointed in one direction I'm pretty sure I could manage that much, at least."

The newcomer just stared at me.

"I'm tellin' ye your aim could use some work," I clarified.

This, unlike my scathing indictment of the male urinary tract and its glaring deficiencies, seemed to incense the man; he puffed up his hairy chest and raised his chin in indignation.

"My aim is perfect," he declared. "I am Dag. Reigning champion."

"Is that so?"

"It's true," Glow interjected, helpfully. "He is."

"Well good for him. Now why don't ye run along and go feel marginally important somewhere else? Go throw an axe or somethin'."

Dag barked a laugh. "You wish to challenge *me*?"

"That's literally not what I said."

"Einherjar! Listen, this little woman wishes to challenge me!"

A small crowd began to form around us at the pronouncement, the onlookers chattering to one another in excitement. I even saw that a few of the einherjar had begun exchanging coins, taking lots on who would win the contest—though I had no idea what contest that might be.

I turned to Glow. "Is that moron deaf?"

The dwarf nodded, his expression oddly sympathetic. "In his left ear. And he's really bad at reading lips. Also reading."

I groaned. "Of course he is."

"So, what are you going to do?"

"What else can I do? It's a challenge, and this is Valhalla. I have no choice. Besides, what's the worst that could happen?"

Glow grinned and clapped me on the shoulder. "That's the spirit. Don't worry, I'm sure you'll do great."

"Of course I will," I replied. "But first, can I ask ye a question?"

"Sure."

"How d'ye throw an axe? Properly, I mean."

The dwarf just looked at me.

I frowned. "What?"

CHAPTER 3

The crowd was hushed as I stepped up to the line some enterprising einherjar had gouged into the floor. The axe handle hung awkwardly in my hand, its unwieldy blade so sharp I worried I might nick myself by accident. Worse, it seemed I had no choice but to throw the damn thing without so much as a practice round; Dag had insisted on it, especially after learning I'd never done this before. He and several of his cronies loitered nearby, no doubt prepared to mock me for what they assumed would be an absolutely abysmal toss.

Funnily enough, now that I'd had some time to sober up a bit, I was feeling pretty good about my chances. I'd thrown my fair share of spears and wielded plenty of swords. Surely throwing an axe couldn't be *that* different.

I hefted the throwing axe and staggered my feet like a sprinter preparing to race, mimicking the stance I'd seen others use, and then raised the weapon above my head with both hands. This had been Glow's advice.

"You'll have more control over the trajectory, that way," he'd explained. "Also, don't forget to breathe. And make sure to use your legs and hips, not your arms. And release the shaft at the top of the motion. You want the axe to at least make it to the target, not go straight into the floor."

"Anythin' else?"

"Whatever you do, don't close your eyes."

I sighed and replayed his instructions in my own head: breathe, use my hips, release the shaft, and keep my eyes open.

Was it just me, or did his instructions sound like something a porn director might say?

I shrugged that off, muttered a number of obscenities under my breath, closed my eyes, and began rocking back and forth on my heels like I'd seen a few of the others do. Once I'd generated a fair amount of momentum, I took in a deep breath and let it out. Then another. And finally, as I let out the third breath, I opened my eyes and released my grip, flinging the hatchet end over end towards the target with all the force I could muster.

The axe struck home.

Sort of.

In actuality, the axe handle made contact with the target first, which in turn sent the instrument of death ricocheting wildly off the wall with a reverberating thud. The terrified onlookers shrieked and ducked as it came hurtling back towards the crowd, its steel blade gleaming with the promise of violence. All except Dag, of course, who was too busy pointing and laughing at me to notice.

That is until the hatchet buried itself in the side of his head.

I winced as Dag collapsed into the arms of his companions, the shaft of the axe protruding at an awkward angle from his thick skull. Of course, the wound wasn't exactly life threatening; you couldn't kill someone who was already dead. Still, I didn't envy the son of a bitch the splitting headache he'd suffer from over the next few days.

"You did that on purpose!" accused one of the handful of einherjar cradling Dag's seemingly lifeless body.

"Who, me?" I pressed a hand to my chest as though wounded. "I don't know what ye mean. I'm just a poor, limp-wristed lass with no hand-eye coordination. Besides, how was I supposed to know he wouldn't duck?"

Dag's cronies grumbled at this but couldn't exactly refute my claims. After all, I was only pointing out the obvious, not to mention regurgitating Dag's own arguments. Of course, the fact that I'd proven the axehole correct *was* a tad galling.

"Anyway, he'll be fine," I insisted with a dismissive wave of my hand. "Just pry it loose and he'll be right as rain by sunrise."

One of Dag's companions raised the man's chin dubiously, and I grimaced to see the einherjar's eyes crossed and staring into space while a steady stream of drool trickled from the corner of his mouth.

"Probably," I added.

The same einherjar cursed and, together with the rest of his fellows, bore Dag like a martyr through the teeming mead hall as though they'd done it dozens of times before. But then, perhaps they had—violent and unexpected deaths were part of the brochure, after all. Still, I waited until they were all well out of ear shot before throwing both arms wide in invitation.

"Now then," I crowed, "who wants to challenge the Mighty Quinn to her next toss, hmm? Anybody?"

CHAPTER 4

With no takers and no desire to linger after having nearly decapitated a man, I ducked past an uncommonly tight-lipped Glow and headed off to resume my quest for booze. I'd only made it a few feet towards the crafting tables, however, before I was halted by the unexpected presence of an axe as it went flying past my face.

Not that I knew it was an axe, at first—not until it struck the nearest target dead center without so much as a quiver.

I froze immediately, too startled to be scared.

"Um, axe-cuse me," I began, turning, "but what the hell was that? Ye could've killed..."

I drifted off as I caught sight of my would-be assailant standing some twenty feet away, her familiar armor scorched and pockmarked, her soot-stained expression wavering between anguish and outrage. Despite her disheveled state, however, the Federal Agent and Valkyrie appeared much as she always had: uncommonly fit, blonde-haired, blue-eyed, and hard as nails.

"It *is* you," she said, tears pricking at the corners of her eyes.

"Hilde?" I asked, flabbergasted. "What are ye doin' here?"

"Me! What are *you* doing here?"

"Uh..." I gestured vaguely at the mead hall in general, though in truth I wasn't sure what to say. To be honest, I hadn't exactly kept track of my comings and goings. "Ye know, stuff."

Hilde gripped the haft of a second axe slung to her hip as though preparing for another throw—one she didn't intend to waste on a stationary target. "Stuff?! Do you have *any* idea what I've gone through looking for you?"

"Um...not really, no. Should I have?"

Hilde spluttered and threw up both hands with an exasperated groan.

"Okay, let's all calm down," I said, placatingly. "Why don't we sit down, have us a little drink, and ye can tell me all about it, hmm?"

"So, it is her, after all," interjected a second voice.

The speaker stepped out from behind my old friend, her scarred lower lip drawn down in a pensive frown. Her verdant cloak was wet around the hem and shoulders, but otherwise she looked much the same as when I'd seen her last, not an hour or so prior. Of course, I could see now that the armor beneath was of far superior quality than the average einherjar's, even if it did leave *very* little to the imagination.

"It's her," Hilde confirmed.

"Then we should hurry. Lady Freya will want to speak to her as soon as possible. Róta, too."

Hilde nodded absentmindedly.

"If it's all the same to ye two," I said, holding up one hand like a schoolgirl hoping to be excused, "I t'ink I'd rather stick around here. See if I can't get me hands on a pint. You're welcome to tag along, of course. The more the merrier."

"Quinn..." Hilde's voice cracked as stared at me.

"What?" I asked, disturbed by the look on the Valkyrie's face and the vague stirrings of guilt that accompanied it.

I really needed that drink.

"Quinn," she said again, "do you have any idea how long you've been gone?"

I snorted. What an odd question to ask in a place like this. To be honest, I hadn't the faintest idea. Valhalla wasn't the sort of realm where you'd find calendars hanging around. In fact, that was sort of the point; who wanted to spend their eternity counting down the days? Not to mention the fact I'd been fairly thoroughly sauced throughout my tenure.

"A couple days?" I ventured. "Maybe a week?

"Try *six months*."

CHAPTER 5

I n the end, I decided to leave with Hilde and her fellow Valkyrie, whose name I later learned was Gerde. Of course, it turned out this wasn't really my choice to make—a fact made clear to me when Hilde threw me over her shoulder like a disobedient child and "escorted" me outside, ignoring my every plea and protest along the way.

And so it was that I found myself fuming in the backseat of a flying contraption that resembled something out of a children's book while my would-be abductors chatted idly up front.

"Oy! Is this a sleigh?" I asked, marveling at the vehicle's workmanship despite myself as we sped across the night sky. My eyes widened. "Wait a minute! Hilde! D'ye steal *Santa's* sleigh?!"

"What? Of course not. This is based on something one of the dwarves designed for Thor and his lunatic goats. Lady Freya has a whole fleet of them."

"Besides," Gerde added, "there's no such thing as—"

"Gerde!" Hilde hissed.

"Well, okay, but strictly speaking—"

"Who gets the credit isn't the point," insisted Hilde. "And I think you know the Allfather would say the same."

Gerde rolled her eyes but didn't press the issue further.

"So, uh...where are we goin'?" I asked in an attempt to break the awkward silence that followed.

"Fólkvangr," replied Hilde. "To see Lady Freya."

"Odin's wife? The goddess? What for?"

Hilde seemed to hesitate. "Quinn, what's the last thing you remember? From before Valhalla, I mean."

I started to reply only to realize I wasn't entirely sure. I shook my head as if to clear it, willing the muddling effects of all the booze I'd consumed to fade long enough for me to recall my whereabouts over the last six months. Of course, it turned out I'd also forgotten the cardinal rule of drinking: what comes around, goes around.

Or, perhaps more accurately, what doesn't kill you can still fucking suck.

Like a sunbeam made of sheer radiation breaking through storm clouds, a sudden, searing pain blossomed behind my right eye, the pressure so great it felt like my skull might crack open any moment to reveal a soppy, lesion-riddled mess that might have once resembled a fully functional brain.

"Hey! Are you alright?"

I barely managed a whimper in response.

"She was drinking for at least four straight days, according to the witnesses I spoke to," Gerde informed her companion in a tone utterly bereft of sympathy. "Heavily, I might add."

"You think she's hungover?"

"I think it's possible."

I moaned and curled up into a ball, one hand pressed to my throbbing eye socket. Hot tears spilled beneath my hand. I heard Hilde curse, though whatever else she had to say was lost to the sound of wind and my pathetic mewling. Just as I was about to throw myself overboard and accept the preferable alternative that was death, however, the pain retreated. I held up a hand to forestall Hilde's concerns, fended off a wave of nausea, swallowed, and let out a ragged sigh of relief.

"Quinn? Quinn! Are you alright?"

"It's okay," I assured the Valkyrie, "I'm okay, now."

More than that, I realized I *was* able to recall something, after all.

"I was visitin' me old home. Aunt Dez's place."

"Forget about that for a second. You really had me worried there. You're sure you're okay?"

I nodded. "Someone had just driven away. A cop, maybe? I remember I was alone. I reached for the doorknob, and then...nothin'."

Hilde cursed under her breath. "I was afraid of that."

"Why?"

"Because, as far as we can tell, that night was the last anyone heard from you until today. Though to be honest it took us a couple weeks to realize you were missing and not just busy tidying up loose ends back in Boston. Leo and the others have been searching for you ever since, even going so far as to reach out to your old friend, Othello. Last I heard, even the Chancery had gotten involved."

Rather than reply, I probed at the flesh around my eye, searching in vain for signs of tenderness. Truth be told, the news that I'd been MIA for six months hadn't really registered at first, and even now I was struggling to grasp what Hilde was trying to tell me. Still, the fact that both Othello—a Russian hacker friend of mine with a very unique set of skills—the Faerie Chancery—an organization run by storybook beings based in my home town—and the bloody Federal Bureau of Investigation hadn't been able to track me down was seriously troubling.

And then, of course, there was the remarkably unsettling fact that I couldn't recall anything at all from that span to make it all worse.

"So what about ye?" I asked, distractedly. "How'd ye end up here in the Norse realm?"

"She came here looking for you," Gerde replied. "And she's been searching for you ever since."

"With Lady Freya's blessing," Hilde reminded her comrade. "She's been worried about you, Quinn. We all have. That's why, when Gerde told me she'd seen someone matching your description in Valhalla..."

"Ye came to find me," I finished for her.

"Exactly."

"I don't understand. How could I not remember the last six *months*? What in the world could I have been doin' all that time?"

But then, I suspected I already knew the answer to that. Or, rather, I knew the answer was within my reach; I could feel it, lingering in the back of my mind like a wound I didn't dare touch for fear it would fester—the source of my guilt and shame. The subconscious reason I'd refused to get sober.

And I saw, and behold a dark horse.

I shook my head and frowned. "Sorry, what was that ye said?"

"I told you I don't know, either," Hilde repeated. "I've been everywhere I could think of, and we've had eyes on Valhalla for quite some time. You must only have arrived there a little while ago for us to miss you. Especially with you looking like *that*."

I glanced down and blinked owlishly at my outfit. The fur-lined green leather trench coat I wore creaked as I adjusted my weight, exposing a two-toned corset with silver snaps and buckles. A pair of red leather pants and boots completed the ensemble. I shivered suddenly, feeling rather like an animated cartoon character who'd just noticed they were running on air. But then, of course, I'd gotten used to the cozy warmth of the mead hall, not to mention the glow of alcohol in my veins.

"She should change before we arrive," Gerde noted, distastefully. "That's no way to dress where we're going."

"Says the holiday pinup girl," I replied, sneering. "Who are you supposed to be anyway, Mrs. Claws? Santa's Little Assassin? No, wait, wait...I've got it. The Slut Who Stole Christmas."

"What was that?"

"Leave it, Gerde," Hilde interjected. "We have more important things to discuss. Quinn, there's a few things you should know before we get to Fólkvangr."

"Too late," Gerde noted, pointing. "We're already here."

Intrigued, I leaned over the side of the sleigh and stared down at the breathtaking landscape below. Spread out before us, bisected neatly by a magical barrier that split night from day, lay a frozen lake in the middle of a sunlit valley. Beyond, bathed in the golden light of dawn, sat rolling hills covered in snow and towering evergreens. And even farther, so distant they seemed hazy and indistinct, rose a trio of snow-capped mountains whose towering peaks disappeared behind the clouds.

Eventually, I realized the little specks I'd mistaken for shrubs and bushes were in fact a herd of reindeer sprawled across the horizon; several of them took off as we flew past, startled by what must have seemed to them an enormous bird of prey.

"Um...since when did this place become a freakin' winter wonderland?" I asked through chattering teeth, clutching at myself for added warmth as gusts of frigid wind tousled my hair and nipped at my exposed skin.

"Here, take this." Hilde offered me a bushy fur cap from seemingly out of nowhere.

"Cheers."

"And yes," she went on, "that was one of the things I wanted to talk to you about. Tonight is the official start of the Yuletide season."

"Yuletide...that's like the Nordic version of Christmas, right?"

Gerde made an affronted noise in the back of her throat.

"Sort of," allowed Hilde. "Though actually it's more the other way around. Pretty much all of the Christmas traditions Regulars observe are really just bastardized versions of Yuletide."

"Like what?"

"Christmas trees. Wreaths. Mistletoe. Carols. Making merry. Elves. The sleigh pulled by flying livestock."

"Presents?" I offered, hopefully.

"To a less commercialized degree, but yes."

"Well, that's not so bad then!" I glanced back and forth from one Valkyrie to the other, noting in particular their glum expressions. "Right?"

"No, you're right."

"So, why d'ye two look like ye made this year's naughty list?"

"It's not like that."

"Then what's it like? Enlighten me."

The former FBI Agent sighed. "It's true. Ordinarily, Yule is a time of celebration among our people. We see it as an opportunity to chase away the long winter nights and to make the most out of what was for many centuries a time of suffering and want. Unfortunately, this year we've had some...unexpected developments."

"Such as?"

"That's none of your business," interjected Gerde, forcefully. Then, to Hilde, "She isn't one of us. If you keep answering her questions, you may as well bind her with oaths yourself."

"I wasn't—"

Gerde held up a hand. "No. I realize you've been gone a long time and have no doubt forgotten our ways, but even you should know better than to share our secrets with an outsider."

I saw the muscles in Hilde's jaw clench, but noticed she didn't argue—which told me all I needed to know about our current situation.

"Ye really don't have to worry about me," I said, raising both hands in mock surrender for Gerde's benefit. "To tell ye the truth, I'm not even the least bit curious what you're up to. I mean, the fact that ye shot down a perfectly innocent question would most definitely raise a few eyebrows among *some* people, sure. But not me. Honestly, I'm not even a particularly curious person. Just ye wait. 'Here lies Quinn MacKenna: she totally minded her own business.' That's what they'll say."

The scantily clad Valkyrie squinted at me over one shoulder, her suspicions written plain as day across her face. Eventually, she sniffed and turned back around. "I hope that's true, for your sake. Anyway, we should hurry. Especially if you hope to be granted an audience with Lady Freya before the Folkmoot begins."

"Ooh! What's a Folkmoot?" I asked, eagerly.

Gerde shot me a severe look that I was only too happy to ignore. Hilde, meanwhile, barked a laugh. "You'll see for yourself soon enough," she assured me as she urged the marvelous sleigh—which I was disappointed to find did not in fact belong to the Big Man, after all—to fly faster with a flick of the reins.

CHAPTER 6

W e left the frozen lake behind and sped onwards, eventually descending low enough to skirt treetops as we wove between the hills. Within a matter of minutes, I noticed an oddly familiar structure jutting from the base of a valley to our left. The sleigh banked wide in that direction, the frigid wind whipping at my cap and burning my lungs.

"Fólkvangr?" I already knew the answer from having visited this place some time ago, but figured it wouldn't hurt to ask.

Hilde nodded.

The tower for which this realm was named stood even taller than I remembered, looming in the midst of the snow-covered valley like a stone monolith crafted by beings who knew nothing of men and their primitive designs. Still, there was something breathtaking about it— perhaps the sprawling network of desiccated vines that swarmed over its limestone exterior like a second skin, or maybe the twinkling chunks of rose quartz that jutted from every third window to form irregular roosts for all manner of indigenous wildlife.

Either way, I was impressed.

Of course, when last I'd seen the tower, much of it had been obscured from view by the realm's lush flora and fauna, including the entrance.

"Oy, whatever happened to Kára?" I asked, reminded of my previous visit and the altercation that had transpired between myself and the young Valkyrie.

Gerde shot Hilde a startled glance.

"She's with Nate Temple, now," Hilde informed me. "Bodyguard duty. Or so Lady Freya tells me."

"Aye? So she found him, then, after all. That's good to hear."

Honestly, I hadn't given much thought to Nate Temple in a while —even excluding my six month hiatus. Now that I had, however, I couldn't help but wonder what had become of him in my absence. Absentmindedly, I checked my pockets for the object his deceased parents had tasked me with presenting him—a gift, supposedly. Something he needed, or would one day need.

It wasn't there.

Not only that, I realized, but I was missing a few other items, as well.

"We have a problem!" I hissed, panicked. "We have to go back. Now."

"Don't be ridiculous," Gerde replied. "We're almost there."

"No, ye don't understand! It's Areadbhar. She's missin'. We have to go back to Valhalla. I must've left her behind somewhere."

"Who—" Gerde began.

"It's her spear," Hilde explained, her tone far too sympathetic for my liking.

"She's more than that. She's a part of me. We're bound. Connected. We aren't meant to be separated. She should be here, now. Flyin' behind us. But I can't *feel* her. D'ye understand? We have to go back."

Gerde looked at Hilde expectantly, and I realized it was my friend who would have to make the call.

"Please," I added.

Hilde sighed. "I don't think your spear is back there."

"What? Where else would she be?"

"Probably wherever you left your armor."

"Me armor? What d'ye mean? What armor?"

"Exactly."

"What..." I froze, realizing too late what Hilde was alluding to. "Me Valkyrie armor."

Hilde nodded.

I blanched and began making various symbols with my hands. Unfortunately, it quickly became clear that not only was I no longer wearing the armor I'd stumbled across while visiting Freya's home in Fólkvangr, but also that I was no longer able to recall the precise signs that would have made altering my appearance possible.

Still, I kept trying.

"I don't understand," I muttered, distraught. "Where is it? And where's Areadbhar?"

Hilde shook her head. "Honestly? I was hoping you could tell me. But I can see from the look on your face that you have no idea. Not consciously, anyway."

"Lady Freya won't be pleased," noted Gerde, who sounded far less smug than I'd have credited under the circumstances.

"No," Hilde agreed, "she won't."

"What's she got to do with it?" I asked.

The Valkyries exchanged glances.

"Tell me!" I insisted.

Hilde handed the reins to Gerde and turned back to look me in the eyes. "That set of armor wasn't hers to give away, Quinn. Brunhilde's armor, my *mother's* armor, was a gift from Odin. She was his champion, not Freya's."

"Lady Freya's," Gerde corrected.

Hilde rolled her eyes. "*Lady* Freya's. Anyway, I can't imagine the Allfather will be happy to learn that the armor his wife loaned you has gone missing."

Gerde coughed. "Understatement."

"Fortunately for you," Hilde continued, "the two of them have bigger things on their minds at the moment."

"Like what?" I asked, more out of obligation than anything. Truthfully, I couldn't be bothered to care; the loss of both Brunhilde's armor and Areadbhar had hit me as hard if not harder than the revelation that I'd been missing for months. And then of course there was the gift I'd been given by Calvin and Makayla Temple. How was I ever going to replace something like *that*?

"Like whether or not Odin is fit to rule the Aesir," Hilde replied.

I nodded, then frowned. "Wait. Come again?"

CHAPTER 7

After displacing a family of terrified rooks and settling atop one of the quartz outcroppings, the three of us abandoned the sleigh and slipped in through an open window into an unoccupied stretch of hallway. I quickly hazarded a look in both directions, surprised to find ourselves alone—especially considering the security wards I'd encountered the last time I was here.

"Not exactly Fort Knox," I noted.

"We got clearance to land before we left," replied Hilde. "Otherwise we'd never have made it past the lake. You won't have seen them, but there were at least a hundred archers camped out among the trees with their bows drawn, watching us as we passed. Lady Freya's men. Very loyal, and very well-trained."

"Really?"

Hilde nodded, her expression grave. "They've started taking a lot more precautions, recently. Not that I blame them. With this many high profile figures in one place and tensions this high, they'd be insane not to."

"Does any of this have to do with what ye said before? About Odin, I mean."

"That is none of your business," Gerde cut in, casting a glare in Hilde's general direction. "You aren't privy to that sort of information. Not yet, certainly, and perhaps not ever."

Hilde made an exasperated noise in the back of her throat. "Do you really think she wouldn't have figured it out on her own, given what we're about to walk into?"

Gerde's eyes narrowed. "What I think is that your loyalties aren't where they should be."

"And what is that supposed to mean?"

Gerde opened her mouth to respond, then seemed to think better of it. Instead, she shook her head and marched off. "We should hurry," she called over her shoulder. "One of the tower guards should have come to greet us by now. The only reason they wouldn't is if they're all preoccupied downstairs, which means we may already be too late."

Hilde watched her go but made no immediate move to follow.

"Who went and rummaged through her stockin's?" I asked once the Valkyrie was out of earshot.

"No one. She's just being difficult."

"Really? Because it seems a lot to me like she's bein' a right cow."

"She has her reasons. Under the circumstances, I can't even say I blame her. I just wish she'd stop making things so damned personal."

"Why? What d'ye do?"

Hilde shook her head. "I'll tell you later. For now, she's probably right. We should get going."

I shrugged and fell back as we hurried after Gerde, the sound of our footsteps hushed beneath the fur-trimmed runners that lined the hallways. It quickly became clear that the tower's interior defied the laws of physics; there were far too many doors, for one thing. They were also far too large, as were the adjoining rooms to which they led. Fireplaces, I noticed, ran rampant throughout, their blazing hearths tucked into every stone wall and casting a warm glow upon many an otherwise windowless room. I supposed I should have been bothered by the otherworldliness of the place, but there was something cozy and welcoming about the tower that put me at ease. Perhaps it was the nostalgic odor of pine that permeated the air, or the innate sense that we were safe here—sheltered from whatever horrors might lurk outside these walls.

"Nice place ye got here," I said as we caught up to Gerde and descended a set of stairs that wrapped around a pillar decorated with the mounted heads of once magnificent animals. "Not exactly PETA friendly, but nice."

"What's a PETA?"

I waved that away. "Doesn't matter. Just a joke."

Gerde shrugged but let her eyes linger over our surroundings. "The tower rarely appears as it does now. Lady Freya's tastes run towards the beauty of nature. Plants and flowers. Bright colors and wildlife. All this...death...is the Allfather's influence."

"If it makes you feel any better," Hilde added, "they do the same thing to the heads of their enemies."

"Don't ye mean your enemies?"

Gerde perked up at this.

Hilde frowned at me as though I'd intentionally caught her in a lie. "Yes, of course that's what I meant. Our enemies."

We proceeded in silence after that, though fortunately it wasn't terribly long before we reached the intended floor. At the bottom of the landing, Gerde flung out one arm, inviting us to pass. Once beyond her, I found myself staring at a pair of staggeringly massive wooden doors the likes of which I'd never seen; branches protruded from each door as though they were in fact some sort of tree, jutting upwards like two sets of antlers curving together to form an impassable barrier. From these branches hung thin silver chains, woven through like tinsel.

"They must have begun early," Gerde observed, joining me. "We're too late."

Behind us, Hilde cursed under her breath. "No, there's another way. We'll just have to use the side entrance and hope no one notices."

"What side entrance?"

"There's a discrete door the servants use to bring in food and wine. It'll be monitored, though, so be prepared to answer a few questions when we arrive. Let's go."

Though Gerde did not appear pleased by the prospect, she did as Hilde commanded, and soon the two of us were trailing the Valkyrie as she wove her way through a half dozen rooms and hallways. Eventually, the three of us ended up in a pantry of sorts, the shelves of which were stuffed with baskets filled with soft white cheese, loaves of bread, and fresh fruit. In one corner stood casks of ale piled all the way to the ceiling, their sides branded with a peculiar sigil shaped like an oncoming wave.

My stomach growled.

"Ye know," I whispered as we crept forward in the dim light provided by a narrow doorway up ahead, "we could just lay low in here and wait for this Folk Music Festival to end?"

"Folkmoot," Gerde corrected.

"Gesundheit."

Hilde shot me a disapproving look. "The answer is no."

"Why not?"

"There'll be plenty of time to eat and drink once we've talked to Lady Freya," she assured me. "Now come on. The great hall is just past that door."

"Ugh." I groaned. "This is the worst Christmas Vacation ever."

"Stop saying that word," Gerde insisted.

"What word? Vacation?"

"Not that one!"

"Worst?"

"No!"

"Then which was it? I can't stop sayin' the word unless ye tell me what it is." I waited with a hand cupped to my ear, my head cocked. "Well?"

Gerde glared at me, her jaw clenched in frustration, and finally stomped off towards the door.

"You shouldn't tease her so much," Hilde chastised.

"Probably not," I admitted with a sigh. "But now I know exactly what gift to get her this year."

"Oh? And what's that?"

"A sense of humor."

CHAPTER 8

W e emerged to find ourselves in an enormous room that reminded me rather strongly of the mead hall I'd so recently left behind—albeit far better lit and significantly less grimy. The former was thanks in large part to the expansive casement window which dominated the westward-facing wall, while the latter could be attributed to the preponderance of seasonally appropriate decorations. Silver banners hung from the rafters amidst boughs of holly and crimson ribbons that spilled to the floor while frosted glass mugs left rings of condensation on charred oak tables littered with peppermints.

Sadly, it seemed I was the only one who appreciated the effect; everyone else appeared far more intent on clustering together and engaging in hushed conversations.

Some I recognized immediately: the fierce Valkyries with their armor stationed at every exit, the einherjar in their thick furs huddled in the far corners, and of course the goddess Freya speaking to a little girl by the window. Others I identified according to what little I'd gleaned of the Norse pantheon over the years. There was Tyr with his missing hand, for instance, regaling some tall youth with a story that involved a great deal of stabbing. Heimdall with his inhumanly pale skin, his gold teeth flashing bright between bloodless lips as he spoke to one of the Vadar. Probably Vidar, judging by the absurdly thick platform shoes he wore.

I turned back to look for Hilde and ended up bumping into a woman. No, I quickly realized. Not a woman, but a goddess dressed all in black whose gilded tresses would have most certainly kissed the floor had they not been braided into so many elegant loops. Her deep green eyes widened upon seeing who it was she'd come into contact with, but she said nothing—not even after I apologized for my part in the collision. If anything, she seemed rather disturbed; she wouldn't stop fidgeting with her lips.

"Is everythin' alright?" I asked, unable to shake the notion that she was in some kind of distress.

Before she could reply, however, a single thunderous clap silenced the room and sent the ethereal creature scurrying away.

The crowd surged apart suddenly, moving to the perimeters of the great hall as though they'd rehearsed it and thereby leaving the center of the room unoccupied. I soon found Hilde at my elbow, guiding me towards an empty patch of wall. Of Gerde there was no sign—not that I was complaining.

"Did I see you talking to Sif just now?" Hilde asked in a hushed voice.

"Sif? Ye mean Thor's wife? Was that who it was?"

"Not his wife. His widow." Hilde's grip on my arm tightened. "What did she say to you?"

I yanked my arm free. "Nothin'! She didn't say a word. Why? What's the big deal?"

"We'll talk about it later. For now, you need to focus. Pay attention to everything they say and do as if your life depends on it. Because it very well might."

"Who's 'they'? And what the hell d'ye mean me life may depend on it'? Depend on what?"

In reply, Hilde pointed to the center of the room.

CHAPTER 9

There, standing several yards apart in the center of the great hall, towered a trio of gods who appeared to share the same face—albeit separated by a matter of decades.

The youngest of the three wore a plain white tunic that gaped open to reveal the muscular swell of his chest as well as a pair of brown leather breeches tucked into shin-high boots. He was tall, clean shaven, and handsome right down to his bones. If he'd been an ordinary man, I'd have pegged him for a celebrity of some kind; the sort who relied on excessive amounts of charisma and more than a little charm to get by.

The remaining two were progressively older and just as arresting in their own ways, but it turned out I didn't have nearly as long to study them before the god in the middle—graying at the temples but powerfully built and practically vibrating with vitality—stepped forward to address the crowd.

"You know me," he said, and I could tell immediately from the gravelly timbre of his voice that he was a serious, no-nonsense individual. A god who put the do in dour, if you know what I mean. "I am Vili, second born son of Borr, and slayer of Ymir. It is I who have called this Folkmoot, and I who shall speak first. Is this acceptable?"

To my surprise it was Freya, stepping out from the middle of the crowd, who answered.

"You are welcome to speak your truth here, Vili son of Borr."

I coughed a laugh into my hand and nudged Hilde. "Did she really just tell him to speak his truth?"

Hilde ignored me.

"I was not born with the gift of a nimble tongue as my brothers were," Vili began, his storm grey eyes narrowed, his expression grave. "In truth I am nothing at all like them. One is young and bold. The other is wise and powerful. I cannot claim such high praise for myself. My talents lie only in the strength of my arm and the loyalty of my friends."

A small cheer went up from the far end of the room—his supporters, presumably, though I had no idea what cause they were supporting. A glance in that direction revealed a tidy cluster of einherjars flanked by several minor gods whose names I didn't know and one not-so-minor goddess whose acquaintance I'd just made. Sort of.

Sif. Thor's widow, Hilde had said. It explained all the black, I supposed. It might even have explained why she refused to speak to me, before. Widows did that, right? A vow of silence? Though...hadn't Thor died a while ago, now? Would she really still be in mourning after all this time?

I sighed and shook my head to clear it, wishing that for once in my life I had more answers than questions.

"And yet," Vili continued, "I stand before you now in recognition of a threat. A threat to our ways. To our continued existence. A threat that must be eradicated if we have any hope of reclaiming what is ours by right."

A murmur of what might have been either excitement or trepidation rippled through the crowd.

Vili held up a hand.

"I am talking, of course, about Nate Temple."

CHAPTER 10

As soon as the words left the god's lips, several cries erupted from the crowd. Some were jeers, though I'd have sworn most were in agreement. I, meanwhile, could do nothing but gape. What the hell had Nate Temple done now? And, more importantly, what sort of minefield had I just walked into?

"You may already know his crimes," Vili called out once the crowd had settled a bit. "But for those who do not, or who have been *blind* to them, I shall list them for you. Firstly, we know he has stolen from us. That even now he lays claim to some of our most valued treasures in his vaunted Armory. We know that he conspired with Loki to free Fenrir, allowing the beast to terrorize our people once more"

His audience shifted uneasily, many of them exchanging worried glances.

"And, most damning of all, we know that he has stolen from us one of our own. That he and his minion have claimed the life of Thor, my nephew and champion of Asgard, husband of Sif."

The golden-haired goddess bowed her head as the room's attention shifted to her, though it was clear she was unhappy.

"From Thor," Vili continued, "Nate Temple has taken possession of Mjolnir, one of if not the greatest of our weapons. And since then? The godkiller has gone on to lop off the head of another pantheon, both literally and figuratively."

"He's not half as bad a public speaker as he's made himself out to be," I muttered.

Hilde snorted. "Wait until you hear the other one."

Vili held up a finger. "Now, I know what you are thinking. You are wondering how this mortal will be punished for the crimes he has committed against us. You wish to know how we intend to repay him and his so-called Horsemen for their hubris in striking at us? And yet, as we stand here today, it is with a heavy heart I must confess that not only have we done nothing to this thief, to this criminal, but that instead my brother has anointed him a member of our war council! Even going so far as to give him a Valkyrie as a bodyguard!"

Several members of the audience balked at this—and not only Vili's supporters.

"Yes! It seems that, in his infinite wisdom, the Allfather who abandoned us for so long has returned without a spine. For what else can we say of his actions, except that they are those of a god who lacks the will to stand up for his own? A leader who does not dare defy the whims of a mortal man, godkiller or no?"

At this, the crowd fell eerily silent. I could tell from their faces that Vili had crossed a line—one there would be no going back from. But then, I supposed that was rather the point; there was certainly no doubt where Vili stood.

"My proposal is simple," Vili said, his eyes flicking across the array of faces in the crowd. "I ask that the Allfather step down so that one of us may lead. One who is willing to break our enemies and remind them of their place. One who will see justice done so that all those who grieve Thor may find peace. One who's willing to do what my brother should have done a long time ago: kill the Temple whelp and display his head for all Nine Realms to see."

"Christ," I breathed, looking to Hilde for confirmation. "He's not jokin', is he?"

"Not at all."

I shook my head at the ramifications of Vili's proposal, too stunned by the staggering implications to speak. What he was suggesting, no matter how bloodless the transition of power proved, was effectively a coup. He wanted to oust Odin for someone more bloodthirsty—or at the very least for someone willing to go to war with Nate Temple. But whom? Vili, himself? Or was he campaigning on someone else's behalf?

Before I could gather my thoughts and ask the question of Hilde, however, a new voice rang through the hall.

"Now, now...let's not be so hasty, brother."

CHAPTER 11

Vili's expression soured. "You will have your turn to speak, Vé."

"Of course," the youngest brother replied, ducking his head. "Forgive me for talking out of turn. Please, continue. I believe you were about to put yourself forward to replace our eldest brother on the throne so you could embroil us in a war over a few missing trinkets and a god very few of us liked against a mortal who has made it his mission to cull our kind?"

For a moment, I—along with everyone else in attendance, including Vili—was rendered speechless. Indeed, it was with no small measure of satisfaction that I watched Vili clamp his mouth shut. When at last he opened it again, his words were laced with indignation and anger.

"My little brother is, as is regrettably so often the case, wrong. If it is the will of our people to see me take the Allfather's place and lead the Aesir, then it is a duty I will gladly accept. However, if another is chosen who is capable and willing to do what must be done, I will not stand in the way."

"Liar," I muttered under my breath. "He just wanted to discredit what the younger one had to say."

Hilde nodded. "You're probably right. Though I'd say that was Vé's plan, judging by his face."

I could tell at once that the Valkyrie was right; Vé's grin was triumphant and his pale blue eyes practically twinkled in amusement.

"Is it my turn to speak now, brother?" he asked after a few moments of silence. "Or did you have something more to say?"

"I am finished."

"Oh, good. I trust you don't mind, Lady Freya?"

I saw Freya purse her lips, but when she spoke, it was without emotion. "You may speak your truth, Vé son of Borr."

"Excellent, excellent." Vé clapped his hands together. "Now, where to begin? Ah, yes. The Temple heir. The mortal who freed Fenrir, tricked Loki, and slew Zeus. A man whose subordinate came to Asgard and defeated the mighty Thor. Leader of a band of newly minted Horsemen. A formidable foe, it would seem. But, perhaps, an even more formidable ally."

A visibly agitated Vili spluttered at this but did not speak. The crowd, meanwhile, shifted nervously as its members muttered to one another.

Vé threw his arms wide and graced the room with a brilliant smile that would have cost an ordinary person a fortune in dental work. "Yes, my friends. Whereas my brother would have you paint Nate Temple the villain, I would urge you to see the untapped resource he represents! Now, you might be asking yourselves whether we've already done so by giving him a seat at our table. After all, a place on our war council and the full time attention of a Valkyrie is no small honor."

Vé inclined his head to those Valkyries gathered, one hand pressed to his breast in acknowledgment. "However, what have we received from this mortal in return? The benefit of his counsel? A decline in possible hostilities? Perhaps. But what about his *allegiance*? How do we know the Horseman of Hope will stand with us? The answer of course is quite simple: we must first prove that we stand with him."

The crowd's reaction was a mixture of shock and dismay, though I could tell from everyone's faces that they were hanging on the youngest brother's every word. I couldn't blame them; Vé had a sweet, honeyed voice that both commanded respect and encouraged listening. The sort of voice that used to pour from radios and enchant audiences well before the dawn of television.

"You see," he continued, "this is something a leader must do, and yet the demands of propriety and tradition have kept the Allfather shackled. That is why he tells us nothing of his motives for abandoning us. That is why he does not confess his whereabouts."

Vé cast a meaningful glance towards the figure furthest from him before shifting his attention back to the crowd. "The Allfather fears what his people might think. What they might do should they disagree with his actions, wise though we can be sure they were. But we cannot have a ruler who is afraid to do what is necessary. In that, my elder brother has it right. The difference between Vili and I, however, is that I intend to bind us closer to a source of remarkable power, not put us at odds with it."

Freya cleared her throat once it was clear Vé had finished. She turned to the last of the three, who had until now remained both expressionless and silent. I paused to study him, dimly aware that I was assessing one of the most notorious beings in existence—a deity whose name was all but synonymous with Hump Day, whose worshippers had raided the known world, spawning countless civilizations in the process.

"You may now speak *your* truth, Odin son of Borr," she said.

The Allfather stared out upon his flock with a single, solitary eye that seemed to see more than the room in which we all stood. The other was covered by a thick leather patch that bisected the mane of white hair that flowed from his head and covered his face. When he spoke, it was with a deep, resounding voice that carried despite how softly he spoke.

"You have heard my brothers speak, and speak well," he said. "I cannot fault them for their feelings, nor find fault in the feelings they have raised in you. It is true, I have invited Nate Temple to join our war council and given leave for one of our own to guard and counsel him. It is also true that I have not sought out an alliance with him, directly. My reasons for doing so are my own and beyond question, as they have always been. Something you all would do well to remember. That is all I have to say."

A general murmur of discontent rose from the crowd, though it was quickly supplanted by an exchange of furtive, meaningful looks. I frowned, sensing immediately the mistake Odin had made in addressing his subjects—a speech bound to alienate anyone who heard it. Indeed, it was precisely that sort of blatant disregard that'd gotten certain monarchs beheaded, albeit in different eras and under different circumstances. Still, I couldn't help but marvel at the inflexibility, the sheer indifference, of Odin's address.

"You have heard from the Allfather and his brothers," Freya announced, her voice cutting through the awkward silence like a hot knife through flesh. "And so concludes the first Folkmoot. Think long and hard upon what you have heard. We shall reconvene tomorrow, at which point you will be allowed to ask questions of them directly. Please enjoy the feast."

As if on cue, the gathered guests began to mingle and disperse, gathering to speak in tidy huddles that might have seemed important had I known precisely whose allegiances lay where. As things stood, however, it was all I could do to process what had just transpired—and what it all might mean, long term.

"What did you think?" Hilde asked, turning to me.

"I'm not sure what to t'ink," I admitted. "I didn't realize the Allfather gig was up for grabs."

"Neither did I. But a lot has changed since I was last here. Odin disappearing for a couple decades upset the balance of power, and now it seems things are progressing faster than they ever have. Nate Temple's influence, I suppose."

"Aye. The man has a way of leavin' behind messes wherever he goes."

"You must know him pretty well, then."

I could tell from Hilde's tone it wasn't an idle question. "Not half as well as ye might t'ink. I had no idea Nate had gotten so involved with your lot, for instance. We don't exactly write each other post-cards. But aye, I know him well enough to guess how he'd feel about what's happenin' here."

"And how's that?"

"We spent some time together in a dream, once."

"Huh?" Hilde shook her head. "No, nevermind. I meant how would he react?"

"Oh, he'd be lovin' it."

"Really?"

"Aye. Everyone runnin' around tryin' to figure out how to deal with him? Worried about what he'll do next? That's how he likes it."

Hilde grunted noncommittally, her expression troubled.

"Listen," I went on. "The one t'ing ye need to know about Nate Temple is that he always thinks he knows best. He manipulates people all the time, then justifies it in his head by sayin' it's the right t'ing to do. And he's usually right. The trouble is, he can't stand it when someone does the same to him. Especially people he trusts. If the Aesir want to stay on his good side, they won't manage it by holdin' closed-door meetin's to decide what course to take. They'd be much better off sendin' the man an invitation. And maybe a written note of apology while they're at it."

"And if they *want* to get on his bad side?" Hilde asked, looking pointedly at Vili, whose back was turned away from us.

I shrugged. "Death comes to us all. Isn't that the sayin'?"

Hilde cocked an eyebrow but didn't disagree with my assessment. Not because she believed Nate Temple could take down an entire pantheon by himself; I doubted either of us had that high an opinion of anyone, frankly. But because she understood what I was implying: no war was ever won without casualties.

"Come on," Hilde insisted, nudging me. "We should speak to Lady Freya while we have a chance."

CHAPTER 12

Freya stared down her nose at me as Hilde explained the circumstances of my sudden reappearance, her expression inscrutable to say the least. She appeared changed since last I'd seen her—less the wild, natural beauty and more the imperious queen. Though I supposed that could largely be chalked up to circumstance; when last we'd met it'd been on the back of the giant tortoise shell she called home, with no one around to overhear our conversation but a few of her most trusted Valkyries. Now we stood in a room teeming with deities, all of whom seemed to be here for the express purpose of deciding whether her husband was fit to lead.

Not exactly a stress free environment, I supposed.

Freya's eyes flicked to my appearance. "The missing armor must stay between us, for now. My husband has too much to concern himself with, already."

"I understand," I replied.

Freya cocked her head. "You truly have no idea where you've been all this time?"

"None."

"Hm. Very well. We will speak more on that, later. I will send someone for you when the feast is concluded so that we may resolve that in private. For now, Hilde will show you to one of the tower's guest rooms. Stay out of sight. We wouldn't want—"

"Wouldn't want what, dearest sister-in-law?"

The rest of us turned to find an unexpected visitor in the form of the youngest son of Borr. Vé leaned against a wooden beam looking awfully pleased with himself. That or he was one of those unbelievably obnoxious, glass-half-full types. Either way, his smile never quite made it all the way to his eyes.

"Nothing you need concern yourself with, Vé," Freya replied, her shoulders tensing.

Vé shrugged. "No matter. And who are you, dear girl? Not one of our worshippers of old, I'd wager. Another one of your projects, Freya? A Valkyrie in training? She certainly has the look."

"Yes, she is," Freya lied. "She just arrived."

"I see. I wonder, how many more Valkyries will you be forced to recruit and send to their deaths if Vili's side wins? I assume you've given it some thought."

"My thoughts on that matter are my own. So long as you remain guests in my realm, you may rely on me to remain neutral. If I couldn't manage that much, I'd never have invited you all."

"A pretty sentiment," Vé replied, "but I think we both know where your allegiances lie. Or, at the very least, where they do not. You know as well as I do what's coming. What's at stake."

Freya scowled but said nothing.

"I noticed your husband has lost his gift for tact as well as his nerve," Vé went on, changing the subject so abruptly that it left my head spinning.

Freya bristled at the accusation. "Perhaps you should accuse the Allfather of that to his face, if that's truly what you believe. No? I did not think so."

"Teasing, dear sister. Merely teasing."

"Don't think Odin does not see through you," Freya warned. "You may have your followers fooled, but some of us remember who you were before Ymir fell. We know from whom Loki first learned his tricks."

Vé barked a laugh. "Of that I have no doubt. I have accused my eldest brother of many things, but being blind has never been one of them. His one eye sees much that our two cannot. Still, what he knows does not overly concern me. It's what he can do about it that matters."

Freya sniffed. "And what are you willing to wager on that score?"

"Oh, everything, I should think."

For some reason, that seemed to startle the goddess. She cleared her throat and glanced back over her shoulder at a young girl sitting at one of the tables with a small retinue of Valkyries. Vé followed her gaze and smirked.

"Oh yes. Temple's ward. A handy bargaining chip, if only the Allfather were willing to—"

"To what?"

This time it was the eldest of the brothers who spoke, spooking Vé, as well as the rest of us, with the menace in his voice. We whirled to find Odin himself standing not a few feet away—impossible to miss, and yet miss him we had.

"You, girl," Odin said, pointing at me and crooking his finger, "come with me. We need to talk."

"I...uh..."

"That wasn't a request," he growled.

I felt my hackles rise but managed to keep from snapping at the haughty son of a bitch—if only just. Maybe I was finally growing up, I thought, as I stepped away from the group and trailed after the imposing Asgardian. That, or maybe even I wasn't so obtuse as to ignore a potentially volatile situation when I saw one. Regardless, I could sense Vé's eyes on me as I departed, his face betraying a sudden and intense curiosity that I wished I could have ignored.

CHAPTER 13

The adjoining chamber Odin led me to was sparsely decorated compared to the great hall, not to mention windowless and therefore significantly darker. An elaborate fireplace dominated the room, its cavernous mouth obstructed by a single log as big as my torso, its flames casting so many shadows it seemed as if the walls were undulating of their own accord. Upon closer inspection, however, I realized the illusion was not due solely to the firelight but to a mural that had been carved onto every inch of the exposed wood, leaving behind a distinct impression of movement as I walked past.

At first glance, the men and women in them appeared to be fighting. Wrestling, perhaps, given the unnatural contortions of their bodies. That is until I noticed how awfully nude they all were. Surprised, I let my eyes wander until I found a figure distinct from the rest—a horned being of unnatural and magnificent proportions, his furry arms and wolffish muzzle raised as though basking in the ecstasy of those cavorting all around him.

"O Come All Ye Faithful," I muttered under my breath.

"Not all sacrifices made to us were bloody," said Odin, who'd taken a seat in one of the two chairs positioned on either side of the fireplace. "Sex was not nearly so taboo a thing in our day, and there was no better time for it than when the nights grew cold and the days grew short."

"I'll take your word for it," I replied, tactfully. "How exactly does one commission an orgy mural, anyway?"

"Why, are you looking to have one made?"

I sensed a note of amusement in Odin's tone and felt a tension ease that I hadn't realized was there. "Not really. I was just makin' polite conversation. Ye know, like how's the weather been...what d'ye do this weekend...who'd ye get to carve your sex wall? That sort of t'ing."

Odin cocked his head. "Funny. But then I was told you would be."

"Told by whom?" I asked, unable to conceal my alarm. "Ye mean Freya? Or was it Hilde?"

For some reason, the Allfather tapped the side of his own head. "I have my sources. Still, I must confess I didn't expect you to end up here of all places. And certainly not now of all times."

"I'm afraid I don't follow."

"Neither do I, and that's what worries me. I am not fond of radical elements, especially not when so much is on the line. And that, Quinn MacKenna, is precisely what you are."

"Um, t'anks?"

"It wasn't a compliment."

I rolled my eyes. "Obviously not. But I don't know what ye expected me to say. It's not like I chose to come here of me own volition."

"Isn't it?"

I frowned. "No. It isn't."

"Very well. Let's say I choose to believe you. What are your intentions, now that you *are* here?"

"How should I know? I've only just arrived. Why don't ye ask your wife? She's the one who invited me to stay."

"Did she, now? And why would she do that?"

I opened my mouth, then shut it. Freya had warned me not to mention Brunhilde's armor lest it upset her husband, and I had to admit she was probably right. The Allfather certainly seemed suspicious enough of me without adding fuel to the Yule Log fire. Indeed, the impression I got from the Asgardian was one of a cross and vaguely disappointed father—not that I had any real expertise in that area.

"What did you think of my speech?" Odin asked a moment later, abandoning his previous line of inquiry so abruptly that it put me immediately on my guard.

"I'm sorry?"

"My speech. I'm asking what you thought."

I hesitated for a moment before responding but ultimately opted for the truth, if only because I hadn't had enough time to come up with a convincing enough lie. "I thought ye made a real mess of it, if I'm bein' honest. Anyone who might have been swayed by your brothers' arguments will only find 'em more credible after everythin' ye said. It was almost like ye were tryin' to antagonize 'em."

"Not almost. That's exactly what I was doing. The question is, do you have any idea why?"

I wracked my brain but couldn't think of any logical reason he might have done it. I told him so, though I also admitted how little I knew the Norse as a people—namely their culture and their values. Hell, for all I knew, they *enjoyed* being told what to do by some old white guy with no consideration for their thoughts or feelings.

Not me, thank you very much.

"We Norse are not so difficult to understand," Odin replied, waving aside my assertion with a magnanimous gesture. "We live to fight, be it in great battles or tavern brawls. To play pranks. To drink. To sing and gamble and flyt. To marry and bear children, though often not in that order."

"Sounds like a pretty solid time," I admitted.

"Indeed it does. In fact, it is. For most. But you see, with hobbies like these there must always be an adult in the room. Someone who can rein in their baser impulses. Someone my people respect enough to make a difficult decision when they cannot. Someone they know to fear when they've made a mistake."

"Someone like ye, ye mean?"

Odin nodded, gravely. "Whatever they may think, I do not rule by popular vote. This is not a democracy. To take my throne, they will have to overthrow me. And that, Ms. MacKenna, would be a very bloody business indeed."

"I see."

"Do you?"

I nodded. "It was a warnin'. Ye weren't tryin' to get 'em on your side. Ye were tellin' 'em what to expect if they choose to side against ye and support your brothers."

"Very good."

I held up a hand. "There's one t'ing I don't understand, though. Why bother pullin' me aside to tell me all this?"

"Because, unlike the rest of us, you have the opportunity to leave before things get ugly. An opportunity I suggest you take." Odin leaned forward in his chair to leer up at me with his single, solitary eye. "You will find no allies here, Quinn MacKenna. Not once they realize who you are. What you are."

I straightened under that heavy-lidded gaze. "And what am I?"

"A pawn in a much larger game."

I bristled at that. "For the record, I am no one's pawn. And, as far as I can tell, the only one playin' games here is ye."

For some reason, this made Odin smile. "I think you'll find I'm hardly the only one, assuming you do decide to stay. Please tell my wife to come see me on your way out. Perhaps I can pry from her the secret you refuse to share."

CHAPTER 14

Hilde passed me a cup of something warm and vaguely alcoholic before gnawing off a hunk of meat from a turkey bone the size of her forearm. We sat at a table in the room she'd procured at Freya's behest, enjoying a tidy little feast of our own while the Folkmoot afterparty raged on. Or at least I assumed that was what was going on; after my private audience with Odin, I'd made myself as scarce as possible before anyone else had the chance to pull me aside and threaten me.

Of course, I still couldn't be sure that's what the Allfather had done. Sure, he'd hit me with a few menacing one-liners, including the ever popular, run-of-the-mead-hall "you better leave if you know what's good for ya" cliche. But then he hadn't really stipulated any consequences so much as implied them, which left me feeling a little like a kid who'd been sent to her room without knowing what she'd done wrong—only that she must have done something.

"Is he right, then?" I asked, leaning back so far in my chair that the front legs came off the ground. "Should I just go?"

Hilde chewed thoughtfully before responding. "Do you want to leave?"

I thought about it. "Not until I know what's goin' on. Why I can't remember anythin'. Where I left the armor and Areadbhar. There has to be a clue somewhere around here. Some reason I ended up in Valhalla of all places. Plus, it sounded like Freya had an idea. Somethin' that might help."

"She might," Hilde acknowledged. "Especially if whatever's causing your memory loss is magical in nature. Like a curse of some kind, or a spell."

"See? There ye go, then. I figure I should at least stay and see what she says. Besides, I'm not entirely sure where I'd even go. Six months."

I settled back and let the enormity of that period sink in, dimly aware that I'd experienced something much like this not so long ago. At the time, I'd just managed to claw my way back to the real world—what the Norse called Midgard—only to find it significantly changed in my absence. To be honest, I couldn't even imagine what had transpired in that time. It felt like I kept leaving everyone behind, and so rarely through any fault of my own.

And yet, somehow I knew this time was different. That, whatever had happened to me, I'd done it to myself. I wasn't sure why I felt that way, only that I did.

"It's an awfully long time to be away from the people you care about," Hilde agreed, though I could tell something was bothering her—the same something that had been bothering her for a while now, if I had to guess.

"What about ye?" I asked, leaning forward and planting both elbows on the table in a way my Aunt Dez would never have allowed. "When d'ye head back? I imagine Leo and the rest will be expecting' ye, now that you've finally found me. T'anks again for that by the way."

"You're welcome. But the truth is I don't know that I will be going back."

"What? Why not?"

Hilde looked down at the table, refusing to meet my gaze. "Do you remember when we first met?"

I did, though I couldn't say she'd made the best impression at the time; Hilde had used a little Valkyrie voodoo to chill the room to test me before then taking me to visit a horrific crime scene—one that featured rather prominently in my more colorful nightmares. Still, that was water under the troll bridge, as they say, and I told her as much.

"Right. And do you remember the reason I joined the Siccos? The reason I gave, anyway?"

"Didn't ye say somethin' about Odin signin' off on it?"

Hilde nodded. "Well, it turns out that wasn't Odin, after all. It was an imposter. In fact, we now know it couldn't have been him. The Allfather was absent at the time, though that didn't become common knowledge until much later."

"Really?" I found myself experiencing a sinking sensation in my gut. Indigestion, maybe? I took another pull from my hot, alcoholic beverage and waited for the discomfort to subside before I spoke again. "Do ye know who it was? The imposter, I mean."

"I don't. No one does. But Quinn...it means my absence was never officially sanctioned. That's why Gerde and a few of the other Valkyries here have taken issue with me. And it's also why I can't go back. Being tricked into abandoning my post is one thing. Willfully ignoring my duties here simply because I've made a better life for myself elsewhere is something else altogether."

"Bullshit."

"What?"

"Don't look at me like that. Ye know what I mean. That's total rubbish, and ye know it is. It's not like you've been on a vacation all these years. You've been chasin' down criminals and helpin' people. They can't punish ye for that."

"They aren't punishing me," Hilde replied, defensively.

"Oh? And how is keepin' ye separated from the people ye love *not* a punishment?"

Hilde appraised me with those glacial blue eyes of hers for a long moment before replying. "Are you sure you don't remember anything from these past few months?"

I shook my head. "Why d'ye ask?"

"I don't know. It's just that you seem...different."

"Different how?"

Hilde took a judicious sip from her own cup. "I'm not sure. But it reminds me of how I was, after Moscow. I wouldn't use the word 'broken' or anything. I wasn't. I just...wasn't myself. Not for a while, anyway."

This time I knew what I was feeling wasn't indigestion, but shame. Shame because it'd been my fault Hilde ended up in Moscow in the first place—my fault she'd spent over a year in a Russian prison being tortured at the behest of a lunatic who'd confused immortality for invulnerability. Granted, we'd made him pay for that mistake, but the Valkyrie still had the scars to show for it.

I'd seen them.

"We'll get ye home, Hilde, no matter what it takes," I said at last. I reached for the Valkyrie's calloused hand and held it tightly in my own. "I swear I won't leave here without ye, understand? Not after ye went through so much to find me. Besides, I've made a bad habit of leavin' the people I care about behind, and I'm done with it."

Hilde smiled and squeezed back. "Then you better eat up. You're going to need your strength. And some sleep. Speaking of which..."

The Valkyrie released my hand, swept my drink off the table, and downed it one smooth gulp. Once finished, she slammed the empty cup down and wiped the back of her hand across her mouth. I, meanwhile, could do nothing except stare in horror at her blatant and unexpected betrayal.

"Oy!" I cried, rousing myself. "What the hell d'ye t'ink you're doin'?!"

"Consider it a favor for a friend. Did you really think I wouldn't notice how hard up you were for a drink all day? Besides, your head needs to be clear tomorrow, which means no more booze and lots of rest. Valkyrie's orders."

I folded my arms across my chest in a huff. "That's it. I take it all back. I'm leavin' ye here to rot, ye miserable cow."

"Now, now, don't be like that. Remember, 'tis the season of giving."

Unfortunately, I couldn't argue with that. Nor did I want to seem too ungrateful after all she'd done for me. And so, in the true spirit of Christmas, I gave her the finger.

CHAPTER 15

I woke the next morning to a pounding at my door feeling anything but clear headed. I'd slept poorly, tossing and turning throughout the night, plagued by feverish, half-remembered dreams rife with both familiar and unfamiliar faces—and all of them covered in blood. I rolled over, bleary-eyed, and groaned a "coming" that took me at least a solid few minutes to honor.

"Who is it?" I asked, leaning my forehead against the door as if it might hold me upright of its own accord.

"It's Róta. I'm here to collect you."

Róta.

The face of a Valkyrie flashed before my eyes: beautiful and formidable, Róta had proven herself more than able to handle herself in a crisis. Even if that crisis had basically been started by me. I rocked back onto my heels, turned the key in the lock, and stepped away from the door.

"Come on in. Freya said she'd send someone to get me. Suppose I should've known it'd be ye."

The woman who opened the door appeared much as I'd seen her last, albeit a tad worn down and frazzled at the edges; errant strands of hair poked out of the tight bun she'd chosen to wear and dark circles plagued her eyes. Admittedly, I wasn't that surprised. When last we'd met, she'd operated in an unofficial capacity as Freya's right hand woman and confidant—a role that no doubt demanded a great deal of time and energy, especially now with so many illustrious guests under her Lady's roof.

Róta studied me with a critical eye, told me to put on some clothes, and within a few minutes the two of us were headed up a narrow staircase that led to Freya's floor of the tower. Yes, I said floor. Mercifully, I'd managed to swap out my previous outfit for something far less conspicuous from Hilde's wardrobe, not to mention a tad less cumbersome.

"Would you stop pawing at yourself, already?"

"Sorry," I replied, though I continued adjusting the woven leather belt that cinched across my waist until it sat comfortably above my hips. Below it poked out the base of a hardened leather bodice, the hem of a crimson tunic that hung like a skirt over a pair of tan breeches, and a pair of soft leather boots laced tight around my calves.

"You look fine," she insisted. "Though you should probably do something about all that hair. A Valkyrie would never leave it hanging in her face like that."

I choked a laugh. "What, ye want me to shave it all off?"

"Maybe not all of it. Just the sides."

"Don't be ridiculous." I drew my hair to one side and held it up to the light, inspecting it for split ends. "Why should I care what a Valkyrie would do, anyway?"

"Because, as of yesterday, that's what you are. A Valkyrie initiate. Congratulations on your acceptance into our ranks."

"Excuse me?"

Róta cocked an eyebrow. "That *is* the lie you told the youngest of Borr's sons, isn't it?"

"Me?! Not on your life. That was Freya's lie, not mine."

"So, you'd rather we tell everyone who you really are, and why you are really here?"

"Why would I care?"

Róta hesitated on the stairs. "Lady Freya told me you were at the Folkmoot, yesterday."

"I was."

"Then you heard the brothers speak. And you realize what the crux of their arguments are? What they want?"

"Aye. One wants to go to war against Nate Temple and his people. The other one wants to bring him into the fold. What about it?"

Róta tutted at me like a child who'd just made a mess of herself. "And it didn't occur to you that you might be loosely considered 'his people'?"

"What? Of course not."

"So you're saying Nate Temple wouldn't ride in here on his white horse to save you if he found out you were being held captive?"

"I'm pretty sure his horse is black. And an alicorn."

Róta pursed her lips.

"Okay, fine," I said, raising my hands in surrender. "The truth is I have no idea. Nate and I aren't exactly close. It's more like...like there's this invisible string that connects us. Like we're always runnin' parallel to one another, even if we don't know it. It's hard to describe."

"Hmm." Róta shrugged. "Well, I still think it's best that the Hird goes on thinking you're one of us. You may not be the bargaining chip they think you are, but it won't stop Vili or Vé from trying to use you, all the same."

I sighed, wishing I could refute the Valkyrie's logic. "Fine. But I'm still not shavin' me head."

"Here, then, take this. It belonged to Kára. I'm sure she would've wanted you to have it."

The hair clip Róta passed over was made of solid gold and fashioned to look like a serpent eating its own tail—an ouroboros, symbol of the cycle of death and rebirth represented in a number of ancient mythologies. A runic inscription rode the serpent's spine and a single ruby chip glimmered where the eye should have been.

"What's it say? This bit here, I mean, with the runes."

"'Don't drop me.'"

"Seriously?" It took me several seconds to realize she'd been making a joke. "Oh, hah hah. Hilarious."

Róta didn't bother suppressing her delighted grin. "It actually says 'live with death in your shadow and you will never fear the dark.' Poetic, isn't it?"

"Very," I replied, repressing a shiver. I hastily handed it back and turned so Róta could secure my hair with it. "By the way, what's that word mean? The one ye said earlier. Hird."

"It's an old word for a court, or a household. We use it to refer to our people whenever they congregate."

"And Folkmoot?"

"A formal meeting. Though in this instance it's been more of a theatrical performance." She tapped my shoulder. "There, all done."

I turned back around. "D'ye really t'ink they're goin' to take Odin's throne?"

"I think they mean to try. But I certainly wouldn't gamble on it. The Allfather may have upset a lot of people when he left, but his absence also proved just how valuable he is in the grand scheme of things."

"How so?"

Róta resumed marching up the stairs rather than reply. However, two flights up, she said, "It's not my place to speak out of turn, but I wouldn't worry too much. Things have a way of sorting themselves out."

I nodded and felt Kára's hair clip tugging gently at my hair. "Will it work? D'ye honestly believe I can pass for a Valkyrie?"

Róta laughed. "It's not exactly far-fetched. You forget, I've seen you fight. Besides, you're hardly high on anyone's list of priorities at the moment. Just keep your head level with your shield, and I can't imagine anyone will bother you."

"What about Odin? He seemed awfully interested in me, yesterday."

"The Allfather won't be pulling you aside again. Lady Freya has seen to that."

Now *that* surprised me. After my little tête-à-tête with his Eyeness, I'd expected at least one more, far less pleasant conversation. "How'd she manage that?"

Róta stopped outside an unremarkable door at the top of the steps and gestured to it. "Ask her yourself. We're here."

CHAPTER 16

Freya and I sat alone in a spacious room heavy with odors of peat smoke and evergreens. The curtains were drawn over the windows, allowing just the faintest sliver of light to dart across the fur pelts littering the floor. The one we sat cross legged upon had once belonged to a bear of considerable size judging by the taxidermied head that resided but a few inches from my right hand. Feeling a smidge guilty, I reached over and patted the creature's head.

There, there Baloo. There, there.

"I thought I told you to clear your mind."

I hastily snapped to attention, careful to keep my expression placid under the goddess's scrutiny. Across from me, Freya wore a far less formal dress. She'd also let her hair down, literally, so that it flowed past her chest and pooled in her lap. In her hands she held runestones—smooth pebbles, each marked with the odd symbol or two—that she cast every so often the way one might throw dice.

She did so again.

"Yahtzee?" I supplied, helpfully.

Freya frowned. "What did I just say?"

"Havin' a clear mind is what got me here in the first place," I reminded her with a sigh. "Besides, I don't see how any of this is helpin'. Maybe if ye were willin' to answer a few of me questions, I'd find it easier to relax."

"I told you already, what my husband and I say to each other behind closed doors is hardly any of your concern."

"It is if it concerns me. But that wasn't what I was goin' to ask about."

Freya poked idly at the stones in front of her. "Very well. What is it you'd like to know?"

"Those stones. What do they mean?"

"All sorts of things, depending on the symbol. Some represent material wealth." Her hand hovered over a small trio of rocks before moving on to another. "Others the obstacles in one's path. There are also some that predict the course that path will take. One's legacy, or spiritual journey."

"So like Tarot cards."

Freya pursed her lips. "A 15th century bastardization utterly stripped of nuance, but yes."

"Well, ye don't sound jealous, at all."

"I am not *jealous*."

I decided to let that go. "So, what then, you're tryin' to tell me future? I thought ye were tryin' to restore me memories."

"I am. But I've begun to err on the side of caution, lately. Whatever has caused this loss of memory seems to have left no mark. At least none that I can see. Which means it may either be an ordinary case of amnesia, or a far more powerful spell than I anticipated."

I nodded in understanding. "And what do the stones say?"

Freya made a face. "Nothing. No matter how many throws I make or how much of my magic I put into them, they refuse to tell me anything."

Well, at least now I knew why she'd kept throwing the damn things. "What happens if ye can't help me?"

"That depends. If it is a spell I cannot break, or perhaps a curse, there are those who we may entreat to remove it. If it's not, then you will remain here and be given time to recover them on your own."

I raised my chin defiantly. "That sounds an awful lot like house arrest."

"Nonsense. If anything, you should consider it a period of convalescence. A chance to recover. This is an offer of hospitality, not imprisonment."

But I was already starting to rise to my feet. "No t'anks."

"Excuse me? Where do you think you are going?"

"Look, I appreciate the sentiment, but let's not kid ourselves. Ye aren't doin' any of this to help me recover the last six months. You're doin' it to find out what happened to Brunhilde's armor. And that's fine. Fair trade and all that. But I won't be kept here against me will. I just won't."

Freya bristled, her expression cold. "Do you really think so low of me that I do this only for my own sake?"

"Why shouldn't I? I only took the armor because I needed it to survive Niflheim. Ye were the one who exploited that need and made me swear to return with Hilde. Well, Hilde's returned, which means our debt is settled, and the armor was mine to lose."

Freya held up a finger. "I gave you a deadline, in case you've forgotten that, as well."

"I remember. So what?"

"Hilde returned only a few months ago. Which means, per our agreement, you work for me."

I clenched my fists as red hot anger began coursing through my entire body. I opened my mouth, prepared to tell the goddess to go fuck herself in seven thousand different ways, but found myself without a voice.

Freya's hand was raised, her fingers twisted in an odd configuration. "Calm yourself. I never intended to enlist you. My Valkyries serve me out of loyalty and love, not fear or obligation. All I wanted was to make sure Hilde was safe and sound. Striking that deal with you was the means to that end, nothing more."

Freya dropped her hand, and I realized I could speak again. "So then ye don't want the armor back?"

"I didn't say that."

"Well, which is it?"

Freya tilted her head and took a moment before responding. "What if I were to swear to you that, in exchange for helping me retrieve the armor, I would gladly allow Hilde to return to Midgard?"

"And why would ye do that?" I asked, suspiciously.

Freya offered me a sad smile. "I am not as cruel as you clearly believe me to be. I know where her loyalty now lies. Where her heart lies. But that does not change the fact that I must recover what has been lost, or else reap the consequences."

"What consequences?"

"That I cannot say."

"But it worries ye."

"Yes."

That I didn't understand. "Are you really that afraid of your own husband?"

"Of my husband? No. Of the Allfather? Only a fool would not be."

"What's the difference?"

Another sad smile. "Every god and goddess has their role to play, Quinn MacKenna, but the truth is very few of us have just one. To some I am a member of the Vanir. To others a powerful witch. Some know me only as the wife of Odin, while others worship me as a goddess in my own right. My husband, on the other hand, is a patriarch as well as a father. In these roles he is kind and patient. Even loving. But as a ruler, as a leader, he can be ruthless. He can be unforgiving, and yes, even petty."

"You're sayin' he'll punish ye for givin' away the armor. As your boss, rather than your spouse."

Freya nodded. "As is his right. I gambled when I allowed Brunhilde's armor to fall into someone else's hands. And no gamble comes without risk."

I let out a long sigh before sinking back to the floor, the flames of my anger fading to mere embers. "Fine, I'll help ye. But I want that bit about Hilde in writin' once we're done here. Now, tell me what to do so we can get this over with."

Freya smiled, genuinely this time. "First, clear your mind. And maybe close your eyes so you're less easily distracted."

"Close your eyes so you're mehmeh meh mehmeh," I mocked in a high-pitched, mulish voice befitting of a child.

"And no talking."

CHAPTER 17

A sudden chill in the air startled me awake. It should have hurt to breathe; it was that cold. Except it didn't, and for some reason that was okay. Indeed, I registered this odd reality the way one might take notice of a passing car with a flat tire or a song played in the wrong key—as though it were an irritant, but hardly an impossibility.

And that's how I knew I was dreaming.

"No, not dreaming. Seeing."

The speaker stood naked and alone with her back to me, staring out at a bleak horizon, the ground around her piled so high with snow it cut her off at the knees. The moment I saw her, it was as if someone had unmuted a television: I could hear waves breaking on a nearby shore and the occasional crack of ice like thunder booming beneath our feet.

Beyond the slender apparition, like a smear across the blue-grey sky, rose a colossal shape, its hazy silhouette weaving back and forth so slowly I couldn't be sure it wasn't merely my eyes playing tricks on me. And yet I knew they weren't. That the thing I saw was not only real, but watching me. Watching us.

Where am I?

"You know where you are," she replied without turning.

I realized she was right. I did know, even if I wasn't sure how I knew, or how I'd gotten here. Of course, it wasn't a place I could name, but rather a place in which something had happened. Something momentous.

Something awful.

"Yes." A brisk wind caught her russet hair and sent dozens of strands fluttering past her shoulder. "This is where it all began. And where it all must end. The place where I cease to exist."

Who are you?

"You know that, too."

She turned, then. Her pale green eyes roamed my face—a face I reached for even as she raised her own hand to do the same, mimicking my actions as convincingly as any mirror.

But then she would, wouldn't she?

"Say it."

You're me.

Strangely enough, however, I hadn't recognized her by our shared appearance, but rather the much the same way you'd know the sight of your own hands or the sound of your own voice. It was instinctive, and immediate.

"Once, perhaps. But not anymore. Though I don't suppose you've made peace with that, yet, or we wouldn't be here."

I don't understand.

"You don't *want* to understand. That's not the same thing."

She was right. Something gripped my mind then—a stab of fear so primal it cast a shadow across my mind. I realized I didn't want to be here any longer. That I didn't belong here. Panicked, I tried to turn and run, but my legs wouldn't work. I was paralyzed and couldn't move.

Help me. Please.

"Of course." Her hand slipped into mine, tugging with an insistence I could not have ignored if I tried—and I didn't want to try, not even when I realized she'd pulled me alongside her to stand at the edge of the cliff overlooking a cold, grey sea.

I can't stay here.

"No, you can't. You should never have come."

I wanted to know.

"But you weren't willing to pay the price. Not yet. Maybe not ever."

My gaze was drawn to her face before being pulled inexorably downwards. Past that pale throat, that prominent collarbone and slightly freckled chest. And it was there, beside her left breast, that I found the bloody hole where her heart—our heart—should have been.

Did I do that to us?

"Who else? Now go, while you still can."

What about you?

"It's too late for me."

And with that, she pushed me over the edge.

CHAPTER 18

I awoke screaming. Pain unlike anything I'd ever known blazed above my right eye, lancing through my brain like a hot poker sprinkled with salt and coated in shards of glass. I wanted to claw my own face off it hurt so bad—to carve my way out of my own skin. But too many hands held me down, stopping me. My throat was on fire as I screeched, my voice shrill in my own ears.

"Quick, give her this!"

Someone poured a foul concoction down my throat and an icy sensation followed, numbing first my aching larynx and then the absurd pain behind my eye. I stopped writhing and started crying tears of relief. Eventually, the hands on my arms and legs disappeared and a frame of familiar faces appeared above me.

"I had a dream," I croaked. "And ye were in it, Scarecrow. And ye, Tin Man. And of course ye were there, Witch."

Freya scowled at me. "Very funny. How are you feeling?"

"And who are you calling Tin Man?" Róta challenged, looking nonplussed.

"I don't know," I admitted, my breathing still labored as I tried to sit up. Hilde was the one who ended up helping me; she held my hand and kept holding it even after I was upright. "What happened?"

"I attempted to use magic to restore your memories," Freya explained. "But all I managed was to put you to sleep. At some point I must have triggered something, however, because you began getting agitated. The fits started soon after that, and that's when I called these two in to help. Tell me, what did you see?"

"Nothin'," I admitted, pressing one palm flat against my forehead. "One second I was clearin' me mind like ye told me to, and the next I woke up screamin' in pain. What was that stuff ye gave me, anyway?"

"Hmm?" Freya glanced down at me, her face troubled. "Oh, it was water from a hot spring in Jötunnheim said to have unique healing properties."

"It tasted disgusting."

"That's not surprising," she replied, distractedly. "The spring is full of dead bodies."

I felt my stomach lurch. "Come again?"

"Oh, the bodies of elves, not giants," she added, as if somehow that made things better.

"Does that mean you really have no idea what's behind this?" Hilde asked of her superior, ignoring the violent gagging noises I was making in the background. "What about those words she kept saying? What did they mean?"

Freya bit her lip and looked away. "I can't be certain."

"What words?" I asked, still clutching at my gut and praying I had a strong enough constitution to handle a tummy full of liquid elf.

"You kept shouting them the whole time we were holding you down," Hilde explained. "The same two words, over and over."

"Really? What were they?"

Róta and Freya exchanged glances.

The goddess cleared her throat. "Dark Horse."

CHAPTER 19

A s I had no clue what the words "Dark Horse" meant and no idea what had provoked me to utter them, I left Freya's private floor feeling dissatisfied to say the least. I'd insisted we try again, of course, but the goddess had proven less than agreeable to the suggestion. Apparently, the elven embalming fluid was a one-off, which meant there'd be no anesthesia should Round 2 go the distance.

"Besides," she'd gone on to tell me, "there are a few things I need to look into before we make our next attempt. I can't say for sure whether or not it was a spell, or a curse. But there was...something. An interference of some kind. I won't risk trying again until I know more."

When I'd asked what she suggested I do in the meantime, she'd pawned me off on Róta with instructions to introduce me to my newfound sisterhood and further solidify my cover as a Valkyrie wannabe. Personally, I felt it was a waste of time and effort. But then, as Hilde pointed out, what else did I have going on?

And so it was that I found myself in a padded room surrounded by a horde of sweaty, half-naked Amazons. Well, not literally; I'd met a true Amazonian once, and none of these women had her predatory grace. But still, they *were* something.

"I haven't been this intimidated since I took that spin class in LA," I muttered, marveling at the display of toned arms and taut stomachs, not to mention their glowing complexions. "I mean, seriously, who do I have to blood eagle to get that skin?"

Róta winced.

"Okay, fine. No ritual sacrifices. But are we talkin' like vitamins, or...? Because I already know it isn't biotin. Wait, let me guess! Is it elf oil? It's elf oil, isn't it?"

While the vast majority of the Valkyries exchanged looks of complete and utter confusion, an exceptionally buxom blonde stepped to the forefront.

"What's *she* doing here?" Gerde asked, her eyes narrowed to slits as she looked me up and down—jealous no doubt that I'd managed to find clothes that weren't three sizes too small.

"My, my," I said in a voice so low only Róta would have been able to hear me. "If it isn't the Whore of Whoville."

Róta shot me a disapproving look.

"Oh, come on. That was funny."

"I think it'd be better if you let me do the talking for a while," she said.

I rolled my eyes but graciously waved for her to proceed.

"Valkyries!" Róta called out in a drill sergeant's voice, turning her attention from me to all those in the room. "Allow me to introduce our newest recruit. Say hello to Quinn. Quinn here was chosen by Lady Freya personally, which should tell you she's not to be trifled with. In fact, after having crossed spears with her once myself, I can attest to that personally."

The Valkyries twittered at that, though I noticed Gerde looked less than impressed. Frankly, I wished Róta had kept that little tidbit to herself. I mean sure we'd fought before, but I wasn't sure it counted what with me being under the influence. And by under the influence I mean experiencing a schizophrenic episode of, shall we say, divine proportions.

"I thought we weren't accepting new blood until the Folkmoot was concluded," Gerde said, addressing Róta directly.

"I suggest you take that up with Lady Freya," Róta replied evenly. "I'm sure she'd love to hear you undermine her authority to her face."

Gerde, cheeks flushed, clamped her mouth shut.

Róta's gaze swept across the room. "Any other questions? No? Alright, then. I assume you're about to finish up drills for the day, yes? Good. I'll be leaving Quinn here to stay and watch. If she has any questions, or requires anything at all, I expect you to be at her disposal. Is that understood?"

A chorus of affirmatives sounded in reply.

"Excellent. Get back to it, then."

The Valkyries, most of whom were armed, began to spread out and break into small groups. Soon, the clatter and clunk of wood on wood filled the air, interrupted only by the occasional shout of triumph or pain.

"Oy, wait a second!" I hissed, wheeling on the Valkyrie at my side. "Ye didn't say anythin' about leavin' me behind."

"Why, were you hoping I'd stick around and hold your hand?"

"What? No!"

"Look, we've been over this. Right now, your goal is to make sure everyone thinks you are who you say you are. That means wherever the other Valkyries are, so are you."

"And what about ye?"

"I have a Folkmoot to prepare for. Unless you'd rather be in charge of securing the great hall and making sure no one tries to kill each other?"

"Well, now that ye mention it..."

Now it was Róta's turn to roll her eyes. "I have to go. Listen to me. I want you to keep a low profile, alright? Watch them spar, pretend to take an interest, and head straight back to your room when they're done."

I held up a hand.

"What is it?" she asked.

"What if I have to go to the bathroom?"

Róta pursed her lips. "Ask for directions. And Quinn? Try not to get into any trouble while I'm gone, alright? I've got enough on my platter."

"Fine, fine," I sighed, flapping my hand at her. "Go on, then. And don't ye worry. I'll be on me very best behavior."

"Now why don't I find that very comforting?"

"Intuition?"

CHAPTER 20

I wandered the perimeter of the room with my hands folded behind my back, ever mindful of the combatants and the possibility of getting clocked by an errant hack or sword thrust. The Valkyries were a marvel to watch. It wasn't just their quick reflexes or brute strength, but the precision with which they anticipated each other—alternatively shielding and counterattacking as a cohesive unit. The warriors sparred for a few minutes at a time before swapping out one set of weapons for another and pairing themselves up against new opponents.

They were on their third rotation when I felt something jab my shoulder.

"Are you really just going to watch?"

I turned and found Gerde, flanked by a pair of Valkyries armed with blunted spears, staring at me. She withdrew her own spear and let it settle to the floor with a thunk, a nasty smile playing on her lips. Between her expression and her aggressive posture, it was obvious to me that I'd pissed her off, somehow. For a moment, I wondered whether she'd overheard my little quip about her outfit. But deep down I knew that wasn't it.

The truth was Gerde didn't like me, and I didn't like her. It happened sometimes. Call it a personality quirk or the clash of certain zodiac signs; it didn't matter. Our disdain for one another was instinctive, if not particularly instructive.

"That was the plan," I replied, coolly. "Why d'ye ask?"

Gerde tipped her head. "Ingrid over there twisted her ankle in her last match. We're supposed to be doing three-on-threes. I thought you might be willing to fill in for her, since you're looking to join our ranks. Or would you rather go find yourself a drink? Don't worry, I won't tell Róta if you cut out early."

A quick glance in the direction Gerde indicated proved there was indeed a Valkyrie nursing an injured leg in the corner of the room. Of course, that didn't mean I was stupid enough to fall for whatever she was plotting. I knew a trap when I saw one. The trouble was I couldn't figure out how she intended to spring it. That, and the fact that I've never been any good at saying no to a fight—fair or otherwise.

"Alright," I replied. "Sure. I'll spar with ye."

Gerde's smile widened. "Glad to hear it."

After a swift removal of layers and some hasty introductions, I stepped onto a patch of padded floor and hoisted the wooden sword I'd been given. It was styled after a broadsword, complete with a metal basket hilt meant to guard the fingers of my dominant hand.

I took a few swings, hoping to get a feel for its weight, and realized it felt much heavier than it ought to. I inspected the blade and pommel, suspicious that it had been tampered with somehow, but found nothing. Indeed, it seemed *I* was the problem. Or, more specifically, my arm. It was fatigued—sore, even. Probably from all the thrashing about on Freya's floor, assuming the faint bruises ringing my wrists and ankles were any indication.

Objectively, the bruises were nothing new. After all, I'd spent a great deal of my life with at least a few purpling my person, whether it be from my extracurricular activities as a rambunctious teenager or my shadowy enterprises as a morally questionable adult. But that didn't change the fact that it had been some time since last I sported any such mark.

You see, bruising was a perfectly normal physiological reaction for a perfectly normal person. Only I wasn't a perfectly normal person. In fact, I wasn't even entirely human. At best, I was a heady blend of abnormal bloodlines and illustrious legacies. And with that distinction came perks. Perks like heightened reflexes, physics-defying strength, and yes, rapid healing capabilities.

And that was to say nothing at all of what I was capable of when I managed to take off my training wheels.

And yet, here I was: physically taxed from an unexpected seizure and fairly exhausted after a bad night's sleep.

"What's the hold up?" Gerde called. "You lost your nerve?"

"No," I snapped, the lie forming before I could consider the alternative. "I'm fine. Great, even."

"That mean you're ready?"

I turned to study the Valkyries who would be fighting beside me, expecting them to be waiting for my cue. Both, however, were preoccupied with their own blades—swinging them about as though to loosen up their hips and shoulders. They were probably nervous, I realized. After all, to them, I was a liability until proven otherwise.

With that in mind, I tightened my grip on my sword, determined not to make a fool of myself.

"Aye. Ready whenever ye are."

Gerde nodded. "Excellent. Ladies, if you would excuse us?"

At first I thought she was talking to her companions, but it soon became apparent she was addressing mine.

My so-called teammates exchanged glances, dropped their blades, and left the mat without so much as a word spoken to me. I stared hollowly after them, my stomach sinking as I realized at last what Gerde had planned. A quick look around revealed the other matches in full swing, which meant there was no one paying attention to our little drama.

It also meant no one would be coming to help.

"Alright, Valkyries." Gerde signaled to her companions. "Let's show Quinn here how we do things."

CHAPTER 21

The two Valkyries struck at once and with the same coordinated effort I'd been privy to all afternoon. The first, a tall brunette with a jaw two inches longer than it needed to be, went high while her companion, a redhead so freckled she was about six tanning sessions away from connecting all the dots, went low. I, meanwhile, could do nothing except stare as their spear tips, blunted but hardly harmless, came flying at me.

In the end, it was muscle memory alone that saved me. I swiveled my hips, removing the target that was my right leg with a quick shift in my stance, and raised my blade to parry the spear headed for my shoulder. It was smoothly done, especially considering how out of practice I was, and yet my recovery was far too sloppy; rather than fall back into a defensive posture, I remained engaged with the brunette and lost track of the redhead.

And so it was I ended up with the end of her spear buried so deep in my belly I swear it tapped my spinal cord. I doubled over in pain with the wind knocked out of me, then dropped to one knee using my spear as a crutch. Hot bile threatened to spill from my mouth, and as I swallowed it back down I swore I could taste decomposed elf.

"Ugh," I groaned, sticking out my tongue. "Tho groth."

"Seriously? That's all you've got? Anyone here could have defended themselves against that attack in their sleep."

I looked up to find Gerde looming over me with one hand planted on her hip. Her outfit was even more risque from this angle; I could see light poking out from between the gap of her breasts, not to mention a healthy amount of underboob. Unfortunately, I was in too much pain at that moment to crack any more jokes at her expense.

"Aye, I'm a little out of practice," I managed to wheeze out. "The last time I had to go two-on-one was when your parents invited me to dinner. What a night."

Okay, so maybe I wasn't as hurt as I thought.

Gerde's cheeks colored. "Stand up."

"Why? So ye can send your flunkies after me again? No t'anks."

But Gerde was already shaking her head. "They won't interfere. I want to test your skills, myself. Though I have to warn you, so far I'm not impressed."

The words stung more than they should have coming from someone I barely knew and didn't like. But the fact was, while I'd managed to do some fairly incredible things in my lifetime, I wasn't proud of anything half as much as I was my scrappiness. Sure, I'd lost fights before, but never without giving at least as good as I got.

Plus, if I was being brutally honest with myself, I knew that no matter how many astonishing abilities I ended up with or how many times I defeated someone or something more powerful than I was, I would always have that chip on my shoulder—that *need* to prove myself.

And nothing about that had changed.

"Fine, we'll do it your way," I said, at last. I rose gingerly to my feet and tossed my sword to the ground, letting it clang beside the others. "But no weapons. If we do this, it's hand-to-hand."

Frankly, I wasn't sure Gerde would go for it. For one thing, I doubted Valkyries had much cause to practice unarmed combat. For another, she was at a severe disadvantage when it came to reach. But, to my surprise, she passed her spear over to one of her companions without any hesitation at all. She instructed them to step back, which they did, leaving us to stare at one another from only a few feet apart.

"Mercy rule?" I asked.

"That's right," Gerde replied, smirking. "When you ask for it, I'll give it to you."

"Weird. That's what your mom said, too."

CHAPTER 22

The Valkyrie lunged at me as if she'd been shot out of a cannon, one knee grazing the floor in a bid to wrap her arms around my legs, lift, and throw me to the ground. It was professionally done—a move so brilliantly executed that, under normal circumstances, I might've let her get away with it out of sheer respect.

As things stood, however, I couldn't afford to let things go quite so smoothly. And so, rather than brace myself as I might ordinarily have done, I thrust my knee directly into her path. As I'd intended, it connected solidly with Gerde's face, catching her so squarely on the nose that her efficient takedown became instead an awkward tackle.

Together we sprawled to the floor, overcome by her momentum, though I managed to fall back with the precise control of someone who'd made a habit of it.

Regrettably, I hadn't anticipated Gerde would recover so quickly. She scrambled over me like a crab even as blood trickled from her nose, fighting for control on the ground. I reared back and drove the heel of my palm into her ear, hoping to disorient her long enough to roll away. But the blow barely registered. If anything, it only seemed to spur the Valkyrie on.

For the next several minutes we pushed and thrashed, each of us trying to outmaneuver the other in a bid for control. Unfortunately, while I may have held the advantage in an upright fight with my longer limbs and martial arts experience, it seemed Gerde had a great deal of practice pinning someone down and keeping them there.

Shocker.

Eventually, with my breath coming in uneven, ragged gasps, I sagged backwards in exhaustion. Gerde pounced on the opportunity and straddled my waist, putting so much weight on my diaphragm I could barely draw air. Indeed, at this point the best I could manage was to buck my hips and hope to throw her off, but that required energy. Energy I simply did not have.

"Give up," Gerde snapped, punctuating her demand with a savage blow to my head.

I raised both arms to shield my face and continued trying to dislodge her, rolling my hips from side to side as though she might simply slide off.

"I said...give up!" Two more blows, this time an elbow to my face and a body shot to my ribs..

I cursed but kept my forearms raised, waiting for an opening. Gerde reared back, preparing to strike another blow, but I got there first. My jab landed, popping her right in that scarred chin of hers. Sadly, the attack was more for show than anything. It had no force behind it, and in fact only made Gerde that much more angry.

She stopped talking altogether and began raining down punches, striking again and again. I managed to block most of them, though a few did get through cleanly. It was the ninth or tenth, however—a jab that caught me just below my eye and had me seeing stars—that proved the back breaker. Or face breaker, I supposed. In any case, after that my defense crumbled and I was left wide open for strike after strike after strike.

"Say it!" Gerde was screaming between pants.

But I wouldn't. Indeed, with each blow that landed, I felt a certain degree of peace settle over me. Familiar faces began flashing before my eyes with every blow, albeit too swiftly to properly contextualize.

I saw a young Callie Penrose's terrified face in a dark alleyway. Hemingway wide-eyed outside a bar. Nate Temple as a child with a young Gunnar Randulf trailing behind him. Odin, looking younger somehow, glaring at me. Calvin and MacKayla Temple. Othello studying herself in a mirror. Then others, less familiar. A huddled couple in cloaks. A stunning blonde in armor. A dead god on a black sand beach.

I might've been delirious, of course—the visions certainly suggested as much—but I couldn't help feeling as though I deserved this beating. That I deserved to be punished, though for what I couldn't say.

And so I stayed silent, and soon the only sound was that of flesh smacking against flesh and the occasional crack of bone on bone. Or maybe that was my imagination; I could no longer see through the blood and the swelling of my eyes. I did, however, notice when Gerde was at last dragged off me, if only because I was finally able to draw a full breath.

My mouth tasted of blood.

"By Loki's brazen balls, look at her face!"

"What were you thinking, Gerde?"

"Someone go find a healer, and hurry! Fly if you have to!"

A window opened then and cold air gusted through the room. I felt someone lay something over me—a blanket, perhaps. A few of the Valkyries were berating Gerde, who defended herself adamantly by arguing that I'd refused to call for mercy. Worse, that I'd started laughing at her. Whether this appeased any of them or not I couldn't tell, and soon a pall descended over the room.

"Clear out," commanded a voice. "I'll wait for the healer. And Gerde? Don't think for a moment that Lady Freya won't hear of this."

After that, the only sounds were the faint scraping of a chair being dragged across the room and the groan of that very same chair as my self-appointed guardian settled into it. Eventually—I couldn't say how long as I may have blacked out once or twice—I heard the patter of footsteps and the faintest swish of skirts.

"My, my. Took things a little too far today, did we?"

CHAPTER 23

I felt a cool hand press itself to my bloody cheek and, from it, a sudden warmth. I curled into that hand with a moan—not of pleasure but of relief. The throbbing agony to which I'd become accustomed began to recede, incrementally, until I was at last able to move my mouth and open my eyes without fighting back a sob. I must've been hurt badly, I realized. Very badly.

"There. That's better."

I reached up to touch my face and found it whole and hale, the shattered bones mended and the split flesh closed. The same proved true of the rest of me, as well, I was pleased to notice. Indeed, even the bruises around my wrists had faded.

The individual who'd healed me rocked back on her heels and stood before offering me her hand. I took it and felt again that warmth coursing through my body until even my exhaustion had vanished. I smiled, unable to help myself.

"That's quite the touch you've got," I told her. "I'd probably have needed reconstructive surgery if it weren't for ye."

"She is the best healer we have."

This came from the other side of the room. There, straddling a chair, sat a slender woman in her late forties—or so her appearance would suggest. The Valkyrie who'd remained at my side, I presumed.

"T'anks for keepin' an eye on me," I said to her.

"No need. I won't bother asking what in the Nine Realms happened between you and Gerde. I'm just glad you're alright. If you want to thank anyone, thank Eir. She used to be one of us, until she discovered a unique talent for repairing broken things."

"This is hardly my first time here," Eir assured me, her smile wry. "Though I will say things don't usually get that out of hand."

"Aye, well, I guess I just have that effect on some people."

"You should work on correcting that, otherwise I'm afraid I'll have to start charging to patch you up." The healer wore an unassuming dress with impossibly large sleeves, and it was from one of these she withdrew a clementine. "Take this. I'm told the healing I perform can have a euphoric effect, but I know for a fact it burns through a whole lot of one's reserves. This should help with that."

I accepted the fruit gladly. "I appreciate it. And the healin', of course. That goes without sayin'."

Eir dipped her chin. "Well, I should be getting back. The feast should be starting soon, which means I'll have my hands full in a few hours curing hangovers."

"The Folkmoot is already over?" I asked, alarmed.

"Nearly," Eir confirmed. "It was winding down when one of the Valkyries found me. Why? Were you supposed to be there?"

"Oh, no. No. I was just curious."

The healer looked at me quizzically before eventually shrugging. "Well, then, I'm off. Do try and stay out of trouble from now on, won't you?"

"I'll do me best," I replied.

"I suppose that's the most I can expect from any of you, isn't it?" Eir waved her own comment away with a grin and swept out the room with the train of her dress hissing along the floor.

"I like her," I said decidedly once she was well out of earshot.

"Everyone does," replied the nearby Valkyrie. "She's a delightful person. Of course it helps that everyone she touches ends up high on adrenaline and endorphins."

I grinned at her. "I know, right?"

The Valkyrie snorted. "Well, now that you've been seen to, what would you like to do? Róta will be busy for the rest of the day running security for the feast, but if you'd like to submit an official complaint, I'm sure she could spare a few minutes."

I was already shaking my head. "No, it's alright. I'd rather keep this between us, if that's alright. Me and the other Valkyries, I mean."

This earned me an arched eyebrow, but then it wasn't like I could explain that I wasn't supposed to be causing trouble—not to mention the fact that I'd been expressly told to stay as far away from the great hall as possible. Besides, it wasn't like I was completely innocent in the whole affair. Had I simply tapped out, I most likely would have avoided the thrashing I recieved.

"I can't promise you that," the Valkyrie admitted. "Rumors being what they are around here. But I expect there'll be some who respect you for it, all the same."

I nodded, careful not to give away how little I cared. The fact was I had absolutely no intention of sticking around playing shield maiden any longer than I had to. As for Gerde, well, I suspected she and I hadn't seen the last of each other.

"Alright, well, I'm goin' to go to me room and lie down," I said as I edged towards the door. "I t'ink I've had a little too much excitement for one day."

But the Valkyrie wasn't looking at me when I spoke, and it took me a moment to realize why: there was a god lingering in the doorway.

A god who knew my name.

"Greetings, Quinn MacKenna. It is nice to finally lay eyes on you in person. Now please, come with me."

CHAPTER 24

As I walked beside him, I realized Heimdall wasn't much taller or broader of shoulder than I was. In fact, the only physical quality he could claim superiority over was his skin: so pale and clear it reminded me of a plaster mold before it had time to dry; it was a wonder he could even tolerate light. And yet he managed to endure the bright, sunlit corridors of Folkvangr without so much as a whimper or a hiss.

"Why do you keep looking at me like that?" he asked, turning his infamous gaze to me. It was a disconcerting experience, to say the least; the sclera of his eyes lacked even the faintest pigmentation, leaving his pupils to float like shards of ice on fields of snow.

"Has anybody ever told ye you'd make a really great vampire?"

Heimdall, guardian of the Bifrost and watchman of the gods, stopped so abruptly he very nearly tripped over his own feet. "I'm sorry, what was that?"

"I'm just sayin', I've met me fair share and not one has skin as white as yours. I mean, they could make a colorless paint and call it Heimdall White and it'd *still* end up dryin' darker than ye."

To his credit, Heimdall simply laughed. "For a moment there I thought you were accusing me of sustaining myself on the lifeblood of mortal creatures."

"Huh? No, not at all. Not that I'd care if ye did."

"No?"

I shrugged. "I had a big problem with 'em a rather long time ago. But I've met a few I don't hate as much, since then. I considered datin' one of 'em. He had a sexy accent. A great ass, too."

"Did he? Well, it's a wonder the relationship fell through with so much to recommend it."

"Wow," I said, drawing out the syllable with both eyebrows raised. "Was that sarcasm? I didn't realize ye lot knew how to use sarcasm."

Now it was Heimdall's turn to shrug. "It's not our strong suit, I'll admit, but just about anything can be mastered, given enough time. And my kind have little if not time."

"Must be nice," I noted, idly. "Is that why ye still haven't told me why ye came to get me? Or where it is we're goin'?"

Heimdall tipped his head as though I'd scored a point, and we resumed walking. "Freya sent me to collect you. I believe she felt I would be best suited to the task."

That didn't surprise me. If Heimdall had one skill that was prized above all others, it was his uncanny perception—a heightened sense of sight that allowed him to play voyeur whenever he wanted. And not just here in Fólkvangr, but across all Nine Realms. The fact that he'd been asked to track me down from so meager a distance, however, was a lot like firing a heat-seeking missile at the sun, and I told him as much.

"Not a bad analogy," he replied, smirking. "But it was necessary. Your presence has been requested in the great hall."

"Me? Why?"

"Because it seems you made an impression on Vé, yesterday. He's done some digging and plans to reveal your identity to the Hird at some point during tomorrow's Folkmoot to score political points. Or so Freya believes."

"Ye don't agree?" I asked, choosing to ignore for the time being the fact that I'd been exposed so soon after deciding to play the part of a fledgling Valkyrie.

Heimdall shrugged. "I believe Vé has a very curious ability to stay out of sight when he pleases. Even mine. It's a trick he passed on to Loki, I suspect."

"Loki?" The mention of the Aesir brought to mind a face shrouded in the shadow of a cave in Niflheim. "You're lookin' for Loki?"

"Not at present. But I do like to keep an eye on him, generally. The powers that be may have called off Ragnarok for the time being, but there will come a day when he and I find ourselves mortal enemies. Fate is inescapable in that way. Though of course you know plenty about that already, don't you?"

"I guess so." I shivered as we passed a drafty window. "So he knows who I am, then? Vé, I mean."

"Who he believes you to be, yes. Though I expect if he knew who you really were, he'd be doing everything in his power to have you thrown out of this place. As would many who find themselves under this roof. Your enemies are, after all, legion."

It was said without an ounce of hostility, and yet this time when I shuddered it was not from the cold. I rubbed at my own arms, wishing I knew precisely what Heimdall meant while simultaneously dreading whatever answer he might give. Fortunately, I was saved having to make the decision by our sudden arrival outside the great hall doors—thrown wide, this time.

"This is where I leave you, Quinn MacKenna." Heimdall tipped an imaginary hat. "I trust you can take things from here?"

"And what if I said no?" I asked softly, loathing how defeated I sounded, even to myself.

Heimdall offered me a sad smile. "I know it may seem little comfort to you as things currently stand, but trust me when I say this is nothing at all compared to what you have already accomplished."

"You're right," I replied, squaring my shoulders. "Fine then, go on and get out of here. There's only room for one deathly pale person at this holiday party, and Mama MacKenna wants to strut her stuff."

Heimdall barked a laugh and bowed his head before departing, leaving me to navigate these choppy, shark-infested waters on my own...though I suspected I was going to need a bigger longship.

CHAPTER 25

I wandered into the midst of the feast with my head on a swivel, and yet I saw no sign of the principal actors in this little Nordic drama. What I did find, however, was a full blown rager in progress. I gaped up at the rafters, many of which were occupied by drunken einherjar kicking their legs back and forth as they tossed wineskins to each other. One fumbled the catch and the bag fell some forty feet to hit the ground with a tremendous splat, resulting in a spray of purple rain.

No one but me seemed to notice, however. Those it doused merely raised their faces to the sky and howled like dogs before clapping mugs and finishing off their drinks. Elsewhere, I saw several versions of classic party games being played, including a rendition of Jenga played with knives and Pin the Tail on the Donkey with live recipients. There were also drinking games, though for the life of me I couldn't tell whether there were any actual rules other than "when I say drink, you drink!"

Indeed, as I skirted the edges of the hall, I found myself forced to acknowledge all sorts of revelry. There was the pair of bare chested Aesir—one male, one female—rolling around on the floor and making out beneath a cluster of mistletoe. The musician who'd clearly ended up over his head and was busy vomiting into his own lute. And of course there were the drunken fools who mistakenly thought themselves acrobats; I actually had to step over one of these as he clutched his shattered leg and cried like a little boy.

And yet, still there was no sign of Freya or the others.

With no idea where to look, I decided to find a nice quiet corner of the hall to sit in and consider my options. Or, rather, the only table in sight not currently being used as either a cup repository or trampoline.

The way I saw it, I only had a few options left now that my cover was officially blown—a cover, I might add, that had lasted less than twenty four hours. The first was to call it quits, hijack a flying sleigh, and hightail it out of Fólkvangr as fast as the north winds would carry me. Of course, unless that sleigh came with an instruction manual and a GPS, I'd still be pretty screwed.

Plus, there was Hilde to consider. The Valkyrie had gone above and beyond in her search for me, and I wasn't about to abandon her simply because I'd been found out. I'd told the truth before: I'd left far too many of my friends behind of late to even consider doing so now.

Of course, I could always hunker down and wait for the storm to pass. Soon, the Folkmoot would end and everyone would return to Asgard, at which point I could enlist Freya's help without having to worry—a tempting proposition, given how little I cared for political scheming. The trouble was, I'd never have been able to endure it; I was a doer, not a waiter.

Which left me with my third and final option: picking a side. Though to what end that would prove useful I couldn't yet say. The truth was I really had no power over Nate Temple or his actions. In fact, I wasn't even entirely sure we were allies. Allies, after all, shared a common cause. They responded to the same rallying cry. If anything, he and I were more like colleagues who happened to know and work with some of the same people.

Setting that aside, it all seemed to boil down to a matter of personalities. There was Vili, whose incessant warmongering had incited the same sort of fervor that had driven more than one country to wage war against another. Vé with his silver tongue and charming smile, saying all the right things without appearing to mean any of them. And then of course Odin, the arrogant Allfather, whose political inflexibility bordered on obstinance.

"Not makin' it very easy on yours truly, are they?" I muttered to myself.

Before I could start compiling a list of pros and cons, however, a newcomer lurched forward and collided with my table. He grunted, swept out a muscular arm to send the place settings crashing to the floor, and promptly shoved a tray full of flagons at me. I took it, too startled to do otherwise.

"Set those down for me would you?" he asked, holding up the amputated appendage he'd used to clear the table. "I do fairly well for myself with just the one hand, but sometimes it requires making a bit of a mess. The name's Tyr, by the way."

I hastily set the tray of drinks down, mindful not to spill the contents of the flagons, all of which were full to the brim with different kinds of booze.

"Quinn," I replied, then hesitated, unsure whether or not I should offer up my last name. After all, Heimdall hadn't said anything about my identity being common knowledge, merely that Vé had figured it out and was planning accordingly.

"Oh, don't worry. I know who you are, Quinn MacKenna. Put her there." Tyr shoved his stump of a wrist towards me as though expecting me to shake, then laughed at my expression. "A joke. Just a joke."

"Have ye been drinkin'?"

Tyr laughed. "Sober as a judge. In fact, that's why I'm here. I need you to try these for me and tell me what you think about each one."

I blinked at him. "Um, why?"

"Because our lovely host has asked me to decide which of these meads should be served at tomorrow's closing ceremonies, and because I think you are a better judge than most of such things."

"Uh, t'anks?"

"You're welcome. Now, why don't we start here with the dark one?"

Bewildered, I did as Tyr asked, distantly aware that I was addressing a being almost as notorious—if not quite as powerful—as Odin, himself. I couldn't be sure how the Aesir had learned my full name, or if this wasn't all some ploy to earn my confidence, or perhaps simply to get me drunk. But then, I didn't rightly care.

After all, a free drink was a free drink.

"Whoa, not so much, not so much," Tyr chastised, tapping my cup and guiding it back down to the table. "Mead is the drink of the gods. One sip of this stuff is enough to affect any mortal."

He wasn't kidding about that; the instant the mead hit my lips it felt as if I licked an electric fence—but in a good way. Honestly, I wasn't sure how to describe it. All I knew was that the moment I set the cup down I experienced a sort of primal, animalistic alertness that no amount of stimulants had ever achieved. The color of Tyr's blue tunic had gone from a drab yellow to arresting ochre, the brown of his eyes now rimmed in orange and flecked with bits of gold.

"Pretty," I noted, breathlessly.

Tyr laughed. "I think you liked that one. Perhaps a little too much! Here, try this one, instead."

This time I took only the smallest sip, knowing instinctively that Tyr's warning was an appropriate one. This time, however, rather than feeling alert, I experienced a wave of nostalgia so poignant that I very nearly cried.

Tyr snatched the flagon out of my hand. "No, no. Not with this crowd. We don't want them reliving their glory days. *Way* too many grudges. Here."

And so the taste test continued for some time until, at last, Tyr passed over a flagon overflowing with cherry red liquid. I took it in trembling hands, my senses overwrought after all the emotions I'd experienced in the last half hour. I took a sip, both dreading and anticipating the result.

"It tastes like joy," I said in surprise, pulling back and eyeing the drink. "But not like ecstasy. More like...contentment?"

"We call that one Yuletide Punch," Tyr noted with a smirk. "And it looks like we have a winner."

"Tell me the truth, Tyr." I set the flagon down, a suspicion forming in my mind. "D'ye come over here just to cheer me up?"

The Aesir shrugged. "It may have occurred to me that you might be in need of a little distraction. But no, not exactly. I came over because I could sense the war waging inside you, and that you had a tough decision to make. Both of which fall under my divine jurisdiction, as it happens."

"You're the Norse god of war?"

"In a manner of speaking."

"What does that mean?"

"It means there are many facets to war. Bloodshed is only a part of it. Camaraderie. Fighting for a common cause. Ambition. Need. War can include all these things."

"So which facet are you responsible for?"

"Justice. Fair play. Honor. Take your pick."

"I see. And what does a god of justice want with me?"

Tyr's smile dimmed. "He wanted to tell you not to be too hard on yourself. That he knows what it is to lose a piece of yourself for the sake of the greater good."

The Aesir raised his maimed limb as if to emphasize his point, oblivious to the fact that nothing he'd said actually *meant* anything to me.

"Am I supposed to say t'anks for that, or...?" I asked.

Tyr opened his mouth, but whatever he'd been about to say was interrupted by a very loud shout from the other end of the great hall.

"Lords and Ladies of the Hird! Please gather round. I have something to say!"

Tyr craned his neck, saw who'd spoken, and swore. "Does he *ever* stop talking?"

CHAPTER 26

Vé, standing on a table in a slightly gaudier outfit than the one he'd worn the day before, held both arms out in supplication as he addressed the crowd he'd called for. I stayed near the shadows in the back—close enough to hear but not so close as to be seen. Tyr had wandered off without a word, his expression grim.

"After hearing from all of you today," he began, flashing his trademark smile, "I have come to realize it is in no one's best interest to create a divide amongst ourselves. Whatever the results of the Folkmoot, we will always be one people; be we Aesir, Vanir, or Jotnar. And so it is in this newfound spirit of camaraderie that I wish to recognize my elder brother, Vili."

The crowd parted as if a spotlight had appeared, revealing the second of Borr's sons. I couldn't see him clearly from my vantage point, but somehow I knew he'd be scowling, his suspicions written clear as day across his face. His reply was gruff.

"Whatever for?"

"For all you have done for our people. After all, it was you, Vili, who landed the final blow against our great grandfather, defeating Ymir. You who thought to fashion from his corpse the world as we know it. I know that we have disagreed, and no doubt shall disagree again, but you are still my brother."

"And what of our eldest?" Vili asked, his skepticism plain. "Why not praise him, as well? Do you think a few kind words will convince me to take sides with you against him?"

"Not at all!" Vé replied, sounding genuinely hurt by the accusation. "The Allfather needs no praise. He is beloved by all for everything he has done, and still does, for us. I merely wanted to extend my gratitude to you. Indeed, I have a gift to prove it."

"A gift?"

"Yes. A treasure we once thought lost." Vé swung out an arm and the crowd parted once more, this time for a slender figure with lustrous golden hair. "I have asked Sif to present it to you as a gesture of good faith."

Unable to see what the goddess was carrying, I edged closer, slipping through the crowd even as Vé continued his speech.

"Behold, brother. I give to you Draupnir, the ring of kings."

A whisper of excitement and awe rippled through the crowd as Sif presented the box. It was wrapped in red velvet and tied with a bow, no different than what one might find under a Christmas tree. Vili reached for it with unsteady hands, his eyes wide as ornaments.

"Is it true?" he asked Sif, his voice trembling.

Sif nodded.

"Brother," he said, looking up at Vé with something very close to adoration, "where did you find it?"

Vé's lips twitched. "I didn't. It was returned to us...by Nate Temple. The man you wish us to go to war with."

Vili's expression soured immediately, though I noticed with some amusement that he didn't discard the present he'd received. Not that I'd have expected him to; according to legend, Draupnir was a ring of solid gold designed to spawn eight more of itself every ninth night— sort of like a printing press, except with gold rings instead of paper money. It was a literally priceless, legendary artifact that any collector —hell, any person—would have traded their right eye for.

"And just how many other treasures does he have of ours?" Vili asked, his posture defiant. "Pieces he isn't willing to return? What of Mjolnir? What of Gleipnir? How do we know he doesn't hold them all?"

Vé seemed to falter for a moment, clearly not having anticipated the swiftness of his brother's counterclaim. "Well, I hardly think the man would be willing to give up one and not the other. I'm sure all he needs is some convincing that *we* are not his enemy."

Still, it was obvious that Vili's words had hit home with some of the Hird: they muttered amongst themselves and seemed far less impressed than Vé had no doubt intended them to be. And worse, he knew it.

"In any case," Vé went on, "the gift of Draupnir is yours. With my compliments, of course. To Vili!"

The toast was taken up by the entire room, although it was half-hearted at best. It seemed the Hird was having difficulty deciding who to support. Which reminded me: where were Odin and Freya? Shouldn't they have been here to see this?

Unfortunately, I was so engrossed in my efforts to locate them that I didn't notice the individual barreling my direction until it was too late, and we'd already inadvertently bumped into each other.

"Watch where you're going!" Vili snapped as we collided. He turned then and, upon seeing who it was he'd run into, narrowed his eyes in suspicion. "Say, who are you, anyway?"

CHAPTER 27

"I ...uh..." I fumbled for words but for once found none within easy reach. "I'm—"

"Because you look like one of Freya's Valkyries," Vili said, eyeing me up and down. "Except you can't be one of them, or you'd be guarding a door somewhere. So, which is it?"

"I *am* a Valkyrie, my lord," I said, snatching at the explanation he'd given me and even going so far as to bow my head in subservience. It was a role that grated on me, naturally, but one every girl learns to play at one point or another. After all, there were only two ways to deal with men in positions of authority: stroke their egos...or threaten to shoot them. And I'd left my gun at home.

"Is that so?"

"But a Valkyrie in trainin', only," I amended, careful not to deviate from the lie we'd come up with in case Vili remained ignorant of my true identity. After all, it wasn't him that Heimdall had warned me about. "I wasn't told to watch any doors, my lord."

"Then why is it you've come? Or were you hoping to partake in the festivities?" Vili sneered at me and spoke again without waiting for my reply. "Did you enjoy the show, then?"

"My lord?"

"My little brother." Vili flung a hand over one shoulder, though in the other I noticed he held his new gift cradled so tightly against his body it reminded me of the way a running back might secure a football. "He does like to indulge in his theatrics."

Well, if *that* wasn't the axe calling the sword sharp.

"Actually," I replied, "I was just on me way to meet someone when I got sort of sucked in with the rest of the crowd."

Whether Vili believed me or not I couldn't tell, but I decided to take my chances and ask him a few questions, anyway. "It did seem rather kind of him, though, don't ye t'ink? Givin' ye a lovely present like that. Is it somethin' special? I've never heard of a Drip Near, before."

"Draupnir," Vili corrected, gripping his little box all that much tighter. "And yes, it is. But you can be certain there will be strings attached. There always are with him."

"Nonsense," came the reply, startling us both.

Vili uttered a string of profanities in an unfamiliar language. "How many times have I told you not to sneak up on people like that?"

Vé offered his brother a condescending shrug. "I can hardly help it if people are too engrossed in their conversations to notice me."

"Maybe we could tie bells on you like we did when we were younger," Vili suggested, spitefully. "That seemed to work."

"Now, now, is that any way to talk to the person who just gave you such a fine present?"

Vili grunted. "I meant what I said about strings. It wouldn't be the first time you used such a thing to manipulate someone."

"I assure you, brother, it is simply a gift," Vé replied, earnestly. "You have my word, or else you may tear out my heart and feed it to the first troll you come across. Though you might get more for it in the dwarven market. You know how little they care for me down there."

For some reason, this seemed to mollify Vili. Looking at them standing there, I could detect a certain camaraderie that had been missing during their verbal jousts—a lukewarm regard that spoke of a centuries' old relationship.

"Perhaps if you hadn't tried so hard to enslave them," Vili replied, a smile tugging at his lips.

"Oh, come now. 'Enslave' is too strong a word, I think. I merely wanted them to work for us."

"Without pay, as I recall."

Vé waved that away as if the distinction mattered little before turning to me at last. "And who is this?"

"One of Freya's Valkyries," Vili replied. "In training, I believe she said."

"Is that so?"

"Aye, that's me," I lied.

Vé's eyes twinkled in amusement. "And yet you seem so familiar. Is it your first time visiting Fólkvangr? Surely not."

I cringed, knowing the instant he finished speaking that Heimdall had been right: Vé knew exactly who I was. Worse, it seemed he'd even unearthed pertinent details, like the fact that I'd been to this realm before—not exactly common knowledge. But how? Who could have told him? Surely it wasn't Freya. Róta, then? No, that made no sense.

Rather than answer immediately, I let my eyes roam the room, desperate for some excuse to get away. And that's when I saw her: the same little girl Freya had been talking to when I first arrived. The one she'd sought out when Vé appeared the last time and made his idle threats—the one he'd referred to as "Temple's ward."

"So sorry, my lords," I said, ducking my head by way of apology, "but I just saw the person who I was supposed to meet with. If you'll excuse me?"

To my relief, both brothers quickly acquiesced and stepped aside, though Vé seemed particularly amused that I should want to escape. Indeed, I'd only made it a few steps when I heard his sickly-sweet voice call out after me.

"I hope to see you again soon!"

I kept walking.

CHAPTER 28

The little girl's name was Alice, and she was an aspiring artist. She was also a big fan of kittens, horses, pie, and a half dozen other things that appealed to children her age. Of course, none of that explained why she sat alone near the window of a great hall in a Nordic realm with a sketch pad in her lap, surrounded by sticks of black charcoal and white chalk.

"My uncle Nate brought me here," she explained, her expression bright with the sort of blind adoration only children could feel for a loved one. "He left me with Lady Freya so I'd be safe, and so I could learn how to See better."

"See? Is there somethin' wrong with your eyes?"

"No, silly," Alice replied, giggling. "*See*. You know, like your mother could."

I froze as an unbidden shiver ran up my spine.

"I remember you, you know," Alice continued glibly, her tongue poking out from the corner of her lips as she worked. Her face was smudged with bits of charcoal and the dust from her choice of medium had fallen to form a halo around her curiously bare feet. "From when you were here before."

"I'm sorry?"

"You were too scary to look at back then, so I hid. But you're not so scary now. Just sad."

"Sad?" I held up a forestalling hand. "Hold on. What d'ye mean I looked scary? Are ye sayin' ye were here the same time I was? In Fólkvangr?"

Alice nodded, though a tiny wrinkle had appeared between her brows—disgust, I realized. "I'd never seen anything wrapped in so much stolen magic. It was horrible. I don't know how you could stand it, being smothered like that."

"I didn't realize I was..." I trailed off, unable to complete the thought as a wave of anxiety and self-loathing washed over me for reasons I simply could not comprehend. Indeed, it felt a tad as though the little girl's words had opened up a wound I hadn't known existed. Especially that bit about stolen magic.

Haven't you ever wondered why you shed your own mind so easily and so often? How come you've swapped one power for another, time and time again?

"It's okay," Alice insisted, reaching out to pat my hand with a grubby one of her own and bringing me back to my senses. "It's all gone now. You're free."

I smiled weakly. "Am I? That's nice."

"You seem sad again. Hey, I know! Would you like to see my picture?"

"Sure."

Alice held up the pad for my perusal, and I was surprised to see she had quite an innate talent for such a young girl—the sort that, with enough time and devotion, could lead to a promising career. Not that she'd have much need for one, given what she could do. Seers were, after all, incredibly rare and sought after individuals.

"See, this is Odin. He looks like he's resting but he's not. He's listening. See that, there? Those are the branches of Yggdrasil. It's the biggest tree you ever saw, only I could only fit these roots here into this picture, and not even all of them because they go so deep."

"What's he listenin' to?" I asked, amused despite myself.

"The tree. It talks to those who know how to listen. I'm a good listener. At least that's what Lady Freya says."

"And what does the tree say?"

"To me? It talks about the Omega War, mostly. Only it doesn't always call it that. Trees don't really talk like us. But you know that already, don't you? You've met one of Yggdrasil's seeds. You called her Eve, remember?"

I jerked back at that, shocked, but Alice went right on talking as though I hadn't reacted at all.

"But if you meant what Yggdrasil is telling *Odin*, she's trying to warn him about all the things that are going to go wrong. This was a long time ago, so some of it's already happened. You know, like wars and stuff."

I nodded, mutely.

"Anyway, you can see from how he's sitting that Odin was a good listener, but it didn't matter. He needed to know more. That's why I made him look a little like Uncle Nate in this picture. Because they both are like that. Would you like to know what he did, then? Odin, I mean. Not Uncle Nate."

"Sure."

Alice flushed and tore out the page she'd been working on to reveal another, this one even more polished than the last. Indeed, there was a sense of grounded reality to the piece that made it hard to believe a child could have drawn it, at all.

"Okay, so, this is Odin again. He's in his disguise with the tall, pointy hat. He says he likes to play dress up so people leave him alone, but I think he just enjoys it. Last week, he pretended to be my butler. Isn't that funny?"

I tried to reconcile the image of the Odin I'd met as this little girl's butler but simply couldn't manage it. Still, stranger things had happened, I supposed.

"That is funny," I agreed.

Alice grinned and returned my attention to the picture. "So that's Odin, and in front of him, that's Mimir's Well."

"Who's Mimir?"

"Some really smart guy, I think," Alice replied, her dainty little brow furrowed in concentration. "His well was magic and it gave people wisdom, which is why Odin was there. He wanted to know things and thought if he could drink from it, the water would give him wisdom."

"Makes sense."

"Right? But it wasn't easy to get there. Odin had to go all the way down past the Norns." Alice shivered. "I don't like them. They're not nice."

"The Norns? D'ye mean the oracles the Norse use?"

"They aren't oracles," Alice corrected sternly, then went on as though repeating a lecture she'd received from someone else. "Oracles tell the future. Only one of the Norns can do that. The other two see the past and the present. They're powerful, but limited. At least that's what Lady Freya says."

"And what about Seers?" I asked, hoping to encourage her to talk about herself to improve her mood.

It worked.

"Seers do it all! But they usually can't See very far in any direction. That's why Lady Freya worries about me, I think."

"What d'ye mean?"

Alice looked at me and something flickered behind those eyes—a profound understanding that belonged in a much more wizened face. "Because I can see further than any of them."

"Oh. Right."

"Anyway," Alice went on, flipping the page to reveal yet another picture. "When Odin got there he met Mimir, who was angry because it was his well. That's how it got its name. Mimir's Well. See how I drew him? All puffed up like that with a crazy face?"

I nodded.

"That's Uncle Nate's face," she whispered conspiratorially behind one hand, her eyes brimming with laughter. "He does the best crazy face."

Now *that* I could agree on.

"You're right, he does."

Alice leaned back. "And then there's Odin over here, standing and pointing because he's telling Mimir he wants to drink from the well. But Mimir says no. Not unless Odin gives him something in trade."

"His eye," I supplied, recalling the story now.

"Aww! You've heard it already?!"

"No, no! I mean, yes, I have. But I much prefer the way ye tell it. Please don't stop."

Alice huffed and spoke through pouting lips. "Well, like you said, Mimir asks for Odin's eye. So Odin gives it to him and takes a drink of water from the well. And that's when he gained the Sight. The end."

"I'm sorry," I said, truthfully. "I didn't mean to ruin your story."

Eventually, Alice sighed. "That's alright. I didn't draw that part of the story anyway. Lady Freya said it wasn't right for a little girl like me to draw someone losing an eye. But I'm not that little. I told her I've Seen way worse stuff than that. But Lady Freya didn't like that."

"I'm not surprised. It's obvious she cares about ye, and no one who cares about someone wants 'em to experience violence. Especially not when they're young."

"I know. But it's not like she'll be able to protect me forever." The girl's face took on that haunted appearance again. "I mean, what happens when she's gone and I'm all alone again?"

I opened my mouth to offer some pithy advice, or perhaps merely some sympathy, but couldn't. The truth was I could still remember being a little girl whose parents had—in one way or another—abandoned her. Sure, I'd had my Aunt Dez for a while, and she'd been as good to me as I could have asked anyone to be. But still, I knew deep down what Alice was going through. And it wasn't something words alone would ever fix.

"Why d'ye draw this one first?" I asked, instead, drawing Alice's attention back to her drawing. "Shouldn't it be last?"

"That's because I knew you were coming."

"I'm sorry?"

Alice tilted her head and smiled brightly at me, her momentary sadness nothing but a memory. "Sometimes you have to begin at the end to figure out where you started. Don't you think?"

My mind raced as I tried to formulate a reply, but before I could a furtive movement near one of the walls caught my attention. I squinted and saw a spectral figure peering at us from behind a large banner, half her body hidden from sight as she beckoned to me. Not that it was difficult to tell who it was; the mane of glittering golden hair rather gave it away.

"Sif? What does she want?"

Alice craned her neck to see what I was looking at and made a sound I could only describe as satisfaction. "About time she showed up."

"Huh?"

"You should go with her," Alice said as she snapped her drawing pad closed and collected her things. "She has something to tell you."

"How d'ye...oh, right. Seer. But what d'ye mean she has somethin' to tell me? She doesn't speak."

"That doesn't mean she doesn't want to," Alice chided me. "It's just that she can't."

"Because of her vow of silence?"

Alice rolled her eyes. "Because someone sewed her mouth shut. Can't you people See anything?"

I shot a startled glance towards the Aesir goddess and found her waving more insistently. What I did not discover, however, was evidence that her mouth had been sewn closed. I turned back to raise this objection, but Alice had already preempted me.

"Here, you'll need this," she said.

In her hand lay a shard of glass unlike anything I'd ever seen. First of all, I couldn't be sure it was glass; its mercurial interior shimmered and shifted through every color like a neon rainbow trapped beneath a frozen window pane. Secondly, it was hot to the touch—something I was so surprised to discover that I nearly dropped it when Alice handed it over to me.

"Be careful," she scolded me, though she giggled as she said it. "This is Bifrosted glass. It's from the rainbow bridge that Grimm broke. You can use it to see through illusions. Just hold it up like this."

Alice showed me what she meant, taking my hand and positioning the shard of glass so that it acted as a lens. Through it, I saw a very different version of the great hall—one completely free of pomp and festive overtones. I also saw Sif and the inky black thread that bound her lips like a living shadow.

I lowered the lens and stared at it, completely awed. It was only then I noticed its peculiar shape—that of a crescent moon, with one end much sharper than the other. I held that end up.

"Yes," Alice said before I could ask the question. "That's what you use to cut through them."

I nodded. "And it's alright if I take this? It seems really valuable."

Alice shrugged. "Not to me. I don't need it. But you *could* come back sometime and tell me a story? I want to hear about that time you met pirates. Or when you fought against the dead men. Or when you learned how to fly!"

Even knowing how she'd come by such knowledge, I couldn't help but gape at the tiny Seer. "But...if ye know about all that already, what's the point in tellin' ye?"

Alice laughed as though the question had been an especially ridiculous one. "Because it's a story, silly. Just because you know what happens doesn't mean you can't enjoy it. Besides, I'm sure I'll like it better the way *you* tell it."

CHAPTER 29

I left Alice and followed the mysterious Sif as she waded through the crowd of revelers, always careful not to stray too far ahead of me and quick to beckon when I lagged behind. Eventually, she pressed herself flat against the wall, glanced in both directions, and vanished through a narrow doorway—one I recognized.

I quickly followed suit, though I did stop to look for Freya one last time. In doing so, I noticed there seemed to be a concerted effort going on—tables being moved, drinks being cleared, and so forth.

"The party must be windin' down," I said to myself.

But then why had Freya sent for me, if she wasn't even in attendance? Had something happened to her? Or was it a ruse cooked up by Heimdall to lure me here? After all, how much did I really know about him?

"Not the time," I reminded myself, clutching at the shard of Bifrosted glass to keep it from shimmering too noticeably as I slipped into the pantry room that Hilde, Gerde, and I had occupied a little more than twenty four hours prior.

I noticed at once that much of the delectable food was missing, as well as over half the casks. I eyed these warily, wondering if any contained the meads that Tyr had made me try. Frankly, I wasn't sure what to make of him, either; to have singled me out of all people, and in the middle of a party no less, was a coincidence I could not abide.

More than that, he'd known things about me—referred to emotions and thoughts he shouldn't have been privy to. The same could be said for Heimdall. And Alice, for that matter, though I could hardly expect otherwise with someone with her talents.

I shook my head and resolved to focus on the moment at hand. The pantry was dim, the air heavy with tantalizing scents, and it appeared Sif's eagerness to communicate with me had run its course; the Aesir stood in the corner of the room with her body turned in profile as though she might ossify and become one with the stone.

"Ye wanted to talk to me?" I asked.

Sif fidgeted with her hair, flicking her eyes from the floor to me and back again. I realized she was nervous, or perhaps afraid. Worse, I knew she'd never be able to tell me which it was unless I removed that troublesome thread that sealed her lips.

"Listen...I want to help ye," I said, addressing the goddess the way I might a spooked horse or a traumatized child. I wasn't sure why, except perhaps that—rightly or wrongly—it was the way I'd been brought up to speak to those suffering from some form of impairment, be it magical or otherwise.

Sif, meanwhile, continued to watch me like a reindeer preparing to bolt.

"I *can* help ye," I insisted. "But ye have to promise to let me. I know what's stoppin' ye from talkin'. I saw it, and I t'ink I have a way to fix it."

I held up the shard of Bifrosted glass, and Sif's eyes went so wide I was afraid they might tumble out of their sockets. She slipped away from the corner of the room and shuffled towards me, gesturing madly all the while at her mouth. I didn't need to be an expert at charades to know what she was trying to tell me.

"Alright, but ye have to stay absolutely still. And close your eyes. I don't want ye watchin' while I cut the thread."

Sif nodded eagerly and closed her eyes, her expression beatific. Like the Virgin Mary, I thought, if the Virgin Mary had been cast as a classic Hollywood beauty with hair made from literal gold. And here I was, about to risk cutting up the Virgin Mary's ecstatic face.

"Jesus take the wheel," I muttered as I raised the shard. First, I double checked to make sure the thread hadn't moved since I'd last seen it. Once I'd confirmed that much, I angled the sharp end of the shard so it hovered mere centimeters from the corner of Sif's mouth. Then, with even greater care than I reserved for shaving my legs, I traced the uneven line of the Aesir's Cupid's bow lips with the jagged piece of rainbow glass.

The goddess lurched back with a gasp, one hand clamped over her mouth.

"Shite! Did I hurt ye?"

But Sif was laughing behind that hand, not screaming.

"You did it!" she exclaimed, her temperament so markedly improved I had to wonder whether she'd been feigning her earlier anxiety. "Oh thank the gods! I never thought I'd be free of the Brokband."

"The Brokband?"

Sif lowered her hand, showing me the silken black thread that had bound her mouth shut. It bore no marks, no sign at all of having been cut. "It's a cursed thread. I have no idea where Vé got it, but you may be familiar with the myth. It was once used to bind Loki's lips. He made a bet with a dwarf and lost his head in the wager, but argued the stakes did not include his neck. Sewing up his lips was the compromise they struck. It was a clever trick, though, you have to admit. He shaved my head once, you know. Loki. But then he had this hair made for me. It's beautiful, don't you think?

I sighed, realizing too late that the Aesir's lips may have been sealed for good reason; she struck me as one of those incessantly chatty types I loathed on principle. But then I recalled the first name she'd mentioned before going off on her little spiel.

"D'ye say the thread belonged to Vé?"

"Well, I don't know about that," Sif admitted. "All I know is that he used it to seal my lips, and then he used his magic to hide it from sight. He's better at illusions than any of the Aesir. Better than Loki, even. Say! How did you know to use that piece of Bifrost like that, anyway? I would never have thought of that."

Not surprising, I thought, as thinking generally required a fully functional brain.

"It wasn't me idea," I replied, instead. "Someone else suggested it. But hold on, why did Vé sew your mouth shut?"

"Oh, right! That's why I brought you here! I almost forgot. I overheard him talking about you, that's why I knew I could trust you. He talked often of his plans without taking notice of me. He thought I'd never be able to tell anyone. But now I can!"

Sif gripped my hand so fiercely my bones grated. I pried it free, though I was careful to keep my expression neutral. "Ye said *his* plans. What plans? Start from the beginnin' this time, if ye please."

"Oh, of course! Forgive me. You won't understand a word of what I'm saying. I have a bad habit of prattling on. Always have. In fact, I remember there was this one time I—"

"From the beginnin'," I repeated, offering my most patient smile to soften the interruption. "Please."

"Right, yes! Alright, from the beginning." She hesitated, one hand hovering beside her mouth. "Do you know who I am?"

"I do."

"And my husband? Do you know who he was?"

"Aye, Thor. I'm sorry for your loss, by the way."

"Oh don't be!" Sif insisted, brightly. "He was a terrible husband. Did you know he used to throw things around when he got drunk, then call for them to return as if they were his stupid hammer? And the lightning! Always the lightning! Do you know how many house fires I had to put out when he was around?"

I coughed to hide a laugh behind my fist. "I see. So what's with all the black you're wearin' then?"

"That was Vé's idea. He was the one who convinced me to spy on Vili, and he said the best way to do that was to pretend to be grieving."

"Wait, ye were a spy? For Vé?"

Sif nodded. "He told me what Vili wanted. That he planned to get revenge on Nate Temple for Thor. But I don't think that was fair. Thor started it, didn't he? My husband was always starting fights. He was bound to lose one, eventually, right?"

I grimaced, reminded rather forcefully of the beating I'd received earlier that afternoon. "I suppose. But I'm confused. Why would Vé have sewn your mouth shut if ye were workin' for him?"

"He said he couldn't risk me talking if Vili found out I was lying. But now I think he didn't want me talking to anyone."

"Why's that?"

"Because he couldn't risk anyone finding out what he was planning. What his true intentions are."

"What intentions?"

Sif frowned. "I've been thinking about it a lot, you know. I'm not the most clever, but I'm not blind, either. It's the ring, you see. The one he gave Vili. The one he made *me* give Vili. It isn't Draupnir. I know because I saw him use his magic to alter it. It's really Andvaranaut. Andvari's Gift. The two rings do the same thing, but they aren't the same. You can see it, if you set them side by side."

"Not to mention Andvari's Gift is cursed."

"Yes! Exactly! So you see, when I saw what he was doing, I had to tell someone. I mean, I may not agree with Vili, but everyone knows how terrible that curse is. And that was centuries ago! It will only have gotten stronger since then."

I arched an eyebrow. "Ye t'ink if Vili puts it on, it might kill him? One of the Aesir?"

"Not might," Sif replied, adamantly. "It will. And that's what Vé wants! He told me so himself before I found you. He said he plans to blame Vili's death on Nate Temple! That everyone will remember it was actually Temple's gift, not Vé's!"

"But why would he do that? I thought he wanted to become Nate's ally?"

Sif hung her head and wrung her hands. "I don't know. But...there were others involved! I've seen them, coming and going from his rooms back in Asgard. Maybe they had something to do with it? Maybe they pressured him?"

That possibility sounded naive, and I told her so.

"You're probably right," she admitted.

"Ye said ye knew to speak to me about this. That ye could trust me. How?"

"Because you're a friend of Nate Temple's! At least that's what Vé said, earlier today, when he was talking to that woman."

"What woman?"

"I don't know. I'd never seen her before. She looked like a Valkyrie, though. But anyway, I thought he meant it in a good way, like you might help us broker an alliance or something. But once I found out what he was really after..."

"Ye thought I might be able to help."

Sif nodded.

I began pacing the room, pouring over everything Sif had just told me. It was a lot to process—perhaps too much to be believed. And yet, it jived with a great deal of what I'd seen and heard so far, such as Vé's flatfooted reaction when Vili brought up the treasures Nate might still have in his possession. It'd seemed out of character to me then. But, assuming Sif was telling the truth, it made at least a little sense.

After all, what better way to ensure his people would side against Nate Temple than to allow the man's greatest detractor to make a few salient points before he died?

Of course, that still left the question of why.

"Alright then," I said, "let's go."

"Go? Go where?"

"Out there, obviously. To confront that weasel and find out what he's really plannin'."

CHAPTER 30

S
if called out to me to stop, but I wasn't in the mood to listen. If anything, I was tired. Tired of the constant gaming and duplicity the Aesir employed at every turn—and not just them, but in fact every pantheon of my acquaintance. What was it about their divinity, I wondered, that made them so damned flawed? But then, perhaps their worshipers were to blame; aspiring to pettiness rather than perfection no doubt had its appeal.

Either way, I'd had enough of their games for one day and was ready to get some answers.

Which was probably why, when I left the pantry for the great hall, I didn't think to stop and look around before shouting to the rafters.

"Lord Vé! I need to talk to ye!"

"Quinn! What *are* you doing?!"

I whirled, prepared to confront the Aesir I'd called for, only to find Freya staring at me with her jaw hanging.

The goddess sat atop a tiered dais in a throne beside her husband's. Odin, meanwhile, set his baleful eye on me as though he might turn me to stone. The pair looked impressive and regal sitting together like that—something I might have mentioned were it not for the extremely awkward circumstances surrounding my arrival.

You see, apparently all that coordinated moving and cleaning earlier had been to prepare a bountiful feast. The formal kind, you know, with proper clothes and social protocols. Protocols I'd breached the instant I stormed into the middle of the great hall and made a scene.

"Well, shite," I muttered. "Somebody could've warned me the party was just the pre-game."

"What is the meaning of this interruption?" thundered Odin from his perch.

To my credit, I took one look at the irascible Aesir in all his finery, bowed my head, and did something I almost never, ever do: I apologized.

"I am so sorry—"

"I wasn't talking to you. *You* will be silent. I was speaking to my wife."

Okay. Never apologizing again. Check.

"I am not certain, husband." Freya leveled as frigid a gaze at me as I'd ever seen, and that included the time she tried to capture and interrogate me. "Perhaps the young woman had too much to drink. Our ways can be difficult for newcomers."

"That is no excuse."

"No it is not, husband. I will have her confined to her room where she can trouble us no more."

"I'm not drunk," I said, defensively. "I was just—"

"Enough!"

Freya flung out one hand, and I felt something cold and unforgiving lash itself about my torso, compressing my chest until it hurt to breathe. I gaped at the brutal use of magic for so small an offense as speaking out of turn. How was I supposed to know the rager had become a formal dinner? And since when were social blunders considered a crime worthy of this kind of treatment?

I gritted my teeth, determined to explain myself even if it killed me. "Ye don't...understand...there is...Vé, he..."

But it was no use. I simply couldn't speak the words—not with Freya's spell sitting like a boulder on my chest.

"I'm sorry, but was that my name I just heard?"

Vé rose from his seat, drawing the attention of everyone gathered as surely as if he'd beat his fist against the table. The Aesir studied me from across the room, a frown tugging at his lips as he faced the monarchs on their imposing thrones.

"I confess I am not familiar enough with this mortal to know why she's chosen to invoke my name, but I am only too willing to hear what she has to say," he offered, graciously.

"Now is hardly the time," Odin insisted, his posture suddenly wary as his lone eye oscillated between the two of us. "Our food will grow cold."

Vé inclined his head. "Of course, brother. I meant no disrespect. I simply thought the Midgardian might have something important to tell us. But I'm sure you're right. Far better that we enjoy a warm meal than portentous news."

Odin's eye narrowed in suspicion, but in the end, it seemed he had no justifiable reason to object. "Very well, she may speak. But keep it brief. We all have endured enough pointless talk today, I think."

"Thank you, Allfather. Your wisdom is truly a thing of legend."

Odin gave Freya the signal, and within a matter of seconds I could breathe freely again. I took a large inhale and let it slow, at which point I noticed Sif standing looking petrified against the wall. She shook her head at me, adamantly, but I'd already made up my mind.

"I'm here to reveal Vé's treachery," I announced, matter-of-factly. "And his plot to—"

"I think you mean Lord Vé," interrupted an imperious voice to my left. I turned to find Vili standing on the opposite side of the hall, a napkin tucked in at his throat and bits of food stuck in his dark beard.

"I remember you, child," he continued. "Though I don't recall you being so disrespectful, or so foolish."

"Lord Vili, I—"

Vili held up a hand. "As much as I would love to hear whatever lies you have concocted, I am afraid it is too late. My little brother has already forewarned me. I know you work for the Allfather, and that anything you say will be to further his aims."

"I assure you she does not work for me," Odin interjected.

"Then why did you seek out a private audience with her yesterday?" Vé asked, mildly. "Or is there an innocent explanation you'd like to share?"

Odin scowled. "What we discussed is none of your business. However, I am willing to swear this mortal does not and has never done my bidding."

"Setting aside whether your promises are worth what they once were," Vili cut in savagely, "I must confess I have no desire to hear whatever lies that creature has to tell us. If you wish to keep the peace in this hall, brother, you should throw her out of here as your wife first suggested."

For a moment it seemed as though the Allfather might push back out of sheer obstinacy, but in the end, he gave the command and a crew of einherjar detached themselves from the wall and advanced on me as though I were a stray cat that needed to be herded. I cast one more glance in Freya's direction, willing her to speak out on my behalf, but was met instead with utter indifference. Indeed, the only sympathetic face I saw as I left the hall was Tyr's—though whether it was sympathy or pity, I could only guess.

CHAPTER 31

I lay in bed with my face turned towards the wall while the two Valkyries I trusted most in the world berated me as if I were a spoiled, unrepentant child.

"Of all the stupid stunts you could have pulled!" Hilde was shouting. "What the hell were you even thinking?"

Róta, however, was far more measured in her response. "What you did could have gotten all of us in a great deal of trouble, and it still might. The two brothers have already begun circulating a story that you were brought here to plant evidence of their betrayal. And the Hird have no reason not to believe them, especially after what you said."

"When I told 'em the truth, ye mean?"

Perhaps it was the tone of my voice that shut them up, or perhaps it was the fact that I'd spoken at all; I hadn't so far—not once since they'd let themselves in.

"What is that supposed to mean?" Hilde asked, at last.

I relayed to them everything Sif had told me in an emotionless monotone, even going so far as to include the events leading up to that moment. I told them about walking with Heimdall and meeting Tyr, about my conversation with Alice and her gift of the Bifrosted glass, and of course about Sif and her thread. When at last I was finished, neither spoke for a long while.

"If it's true—" Hilde began.

"It doesn't matter," Róta interrupted.

"Of course it matters! If Quinn is right—"

"No," I said, siding at once with the senior Valkyrie. "She's right. Anythin' I say now will be discredited immediately. Vé saw to that when he turned Vili against me."

Hilde grunted. "Well, what about Sif? She could testify that you were telling the truth."

"And implicate herself?" I shook my head. "I should have thought it through. Of course she wouldn't say anythin'. She'd have to admit to everyone how much she loathed her husband, not to mention the fact that she'd been spyin' on one of her own."

"She'd be ostracized," Róta acknowledged. "At least for a couple hundred years, until people forgot. But that's an awful long time to be despised."

"So you're saying there's nothing we can do?" Hilde began pacing the room. "I refuse to believe that."

"There is one thing," Róta ventured, though it sounded to me like she regretted saying it the moment the words left her mouth.

"What?" Hilde asked.

"Well, all we have right now is an accusation, when what we actually need is proof. If we had the real Draupnir, for example, we might be able to persuade Vili and the rest of the Hird of Vé's true intentions, whatever they may be."

Hilde grunted. "Isn't it obvious? He wants to be in charge. He may think he's special, but I've met plenty of men like him in Midgard. *Bureaucrats.*" She practically spat the word. "All those types care about is being in charge. The real question is, where is the real Draupnir? Do you think he's got it? Vé, I mean?"

"I think no illusion is perfect, not even his," Róta replied. "He'd need the original to make it look real. So yes, if I had to guess, I'd say Vé has Draupnir in his possession."

"Is there any way to verify..."

"It's possible, but we'd need..."

"We can..."

"That's not a bad idea, but..."

I continued to lie still, their words like the incessant drone of insects on a summer's evening. Finally, I spoke.

"What's the point?"

Both Valkyries fell immediately silent.

"Quinn?" Hilde asked.

"I mean, who cares?" I went on. "It's not like it's our job to protect these people from themselves, so why risk our necks to do it?"

"Quinn," Róta said, "if this is about Lady Freya—"

"Whatever you're about to say, I don't want to hear it," I snarled. "I really, really don't."

"She was trying to protect you."

"The hell she was!" I shot up to a sitting position and leveled a single, accusatory finger at the Valkyrie. "Ye weren't the one she used her magic on! Ye weren't the one she let be dragged out of the room like a criminal. Damnit, Róta, I didn't ask to be here!"

I slammed my fist against the wall and bit off a curse, dimly aware that I may very well have broken a bone in my hand out of sheer stupidity. Unfortunately, I was too angry to care. "I'm done, d'ye hear me?! Done. I don't care anymore. Ye can all go kill each other for all it matters to me. In fact, from now on, I won't lift a single finger to stop ye. Alright? So go on. Get out."

"This is all my fault."

I froze, startled almost as much by the admission itself as the person who said it.

"I should never have cast that spell," Freya admitted as she slipped through the open door and shuffled into the room. "I simply couldn't risk letting you speak without knowing what you'd say. Especially not in front of my husband."

The two Valkyries exchanged looks.

"He warned me yesterday to keep you out of our affairs until the Folkmoot was concluded, you see," Freya went on. "But when I heard Vé was looking for you, that he knew who you were, I thought it would be better to keep you by my side. Only I was called away by... other business."

"Lady Freya—" Róta began.

The goddess cut her off with a gesture. "I heard everything through the door. I understand now why Quinn felt she had to intervene. And I understand, too, how she feels. I betrayed your faith in me, Quinn, and for that I am truly, deeply sorry."

I swallowed past the sudden lump in my throat, my anger still simmering but no longer boiling. "So...what are ye goin' to do about Vé?"

"There is nothing I can do, I'm afraid," the goddess replied with a sigh. "Róta is right. Without Sif's testimony or some other kind of proof, it would be your word against his."

"Even if they inspected the ring Vé gave to Vili?" I asked.

Freya shook her head. "To even consider doing so would be to give credence to the possibility that one brother intended to harm the other, which would be far too serious an allegation. Also, I am not so sure Vé's illusion spell would be so easily broken. None of us noticed the one he cast to conceal the Brokband, after all."

"What about this?" I drew the shard of Bifrosted glass out from under my pillow and held it out for Freya's inspection. "Couldn't they use it to see the truth?"

"I'm afraid using one magical object to disprove the veracity of the other would be poorly received. Vé need only claim your glass is the fake, and we would be right back where we started."

"Then it *is* hopeless," I said, regretfully. "That sleazeball is really goin' to get away with it."

But Freya was already shaking her head. "Not necessarily. I think perhaps we should revisit the idea of locating the true Draupnir. But first, I need to be sure about something."

"Be sure about what?"

"About whether or not you truly wish to be a part of this. I only ask because what you said before was true. This is not your battle to fight, and we are not your people to save."

I considered her words carefully.

"I want to do it."

"And may I ask why?"

"Ye want the truth?"

Freya nodded. "Please."

"Well, to be honest, I didn't even really mean what I said before. I was just angry. I tend to lash out when I get angry." I glanced down at my throbbing hand and raised it to prove my point. "But, more than that...more than anythin', really...I want to see that piece of shite suffer."

Freya's eyes widened. "You mean Vé?"

"Aye. I mean, how can ye look at that smug bastard's face and *not* want to punch it?"

My three companions exchanged looks and, without warning or explanation, began laughing uproariously.

"What?! I'm bein' serious!"

"We know," Hilde confessed, dabbing at her eyes. "That's the funny part."

"Whatever," I huffed. "So, are we doin' this, or aren't we?"

"Jokes aside." Freya held up a hand and we all fell silent. "I'm afraid I can't be seen helping you. Officially speaking, I'm not allowed to take sides, which means I can't risk being implicated in whatever you decide to do. What I can offer, however, is information...and perhaps a little guidance."

"We'll take all the help we can get," I affirmed.

"Very well. Now then, first things first, do any of you have experience breaking and entering?"

"Oh yes," I said, raising my hand with all the aplomb of a woman who'd committed many, many felonies. "That would be me."

CHAPTER 32

For the rest of that day it was like Christmas had come early. After all, what else could I ask for if not to spend hours plotting a proper heist? I couldn't speak for the others, of course; Róta took to it well enough, but as a law enforcement agent, Hilde had proven a tad less enthusiastic—specifically in regards to the use of explosives, which was an idea I'd floated early on.

Though Freya hadn't been too fond of that suggestion either, come to think of it.

In any case, by the next morning, we had a scheme in place and needed only an hour or two to prepare. Each of us had our roles to play. Freya's was to host a private gathering of the Aesir's most influential members—a ploy that was bound to lure a meddler like Vé away from his rooms.

Róta had a simpler task, and it was one she'd already performed the night before: rearranging the Valkyrie's schedule to provide a ten minute window in which the doors would remain unguarded. It wasn't long, but anything more than that and we risked Freya being charged with complicity should I be caught.

That's right: the role of thief in our little caper was to be played by yours truly. Not that this came as a surprise to me. I was, after all, immensely qualified.

And finally there was Hilde, who would act as lookout and, should the need arise, problem-solver. If the guards arrived early, for instance, it was her job to distract them—and make enough noise in the process that I'd be forewarned. If Vé returned or someone else approached, she could pretend to be a guard and come up with some excuse to keep them out long enough for me to either hide or make my escape.

All in all, I thought it was a solid blueprint for a heist, albeit a tad short of explosions and elaborate disguises for my tastes.

"Ye ready?" I whispered to Hilde. The two of us hid around the corner from Vé's rooms, all three of which were joined along the same stretch of hallway. The Aesir himself had already departed, going off in the opposite direction towards the great hall some five minutes prior.

"Have they gone?"

"Any second now."

The two Valkyries guarding the corridor glanced back and forth in either direction the way one might before crossing the street, clearly wondering how much longer it would be before their replacements showed up. When they did not, the pair conferred for a moment before finally abandoning their post, their idle chatter sounding fainter and fainter as they departed.

"They're gone," I said. "Wish me luck."

"Break someone's leg."

I grinned, slipped into the hallway, and—as was my habit whenever I was about to do something illegal—walked as casually as you please until I reached the first of the three doors.

Fun fact about committing a crime: unless it's a foot race and you happen to be a world class sprinter, you should never run. Running is a sign of guilt—a reaction far more likely to get you caught than simply pretending you'd done nothing wrong in the first place. Besides, it'll make your lawyer's life a whole lot easier.

Trust me.

I knocked on the door with a heavy fist just to be sure there was no one else inside before trying the door handle. It wouldn't budge. I quickly went down the line, checking all three handles just in case. No dice.

Fortunately, we'd prepared for such an eventuality.

I produced the key Freya had given me, fit it into the nearest lock, and opened the door. Then, to make certain no one would find evidence of it on my person should I be searched, I tossed the key to the end of the hall where Hilde would be able to retrieve it. That done, I quietly slipped inside.

The room I entered was a bedroom and not so different from my own: the same four-poster bed, the same stone floors and animal pelt rug, even the same nightstands fashioned from animal horn and sandalwood. Indeed, the only notable difference between the two was that this room fed into two others—the first a living space and the second a private kitchen. That, and the presence of a large wooden chest sealed shut by an obnoxiously thick padlock from a bygone era.

Fully aware that time was of the essence, I performed a hasty check of all three rooms to ensure the ring was not lying out in the open somewhere—not that I expected Vé to be as irresponsible as all that.

Again, no luck.

Switching gears, I began searching each of the rooms, beginning with the living area as it was the least likely of the three; there were far fewer items of furniture in that space which might conventionally hide a ring. I quickly nosed around the wooden coffee table, lifted and shook the wicker chairs, and finally opened every dresser drawer. I even shoved an iron poker into the fireplace, probing at the ashes for that tell-tale glint of gold.

Nothing.

The kitchen, regrettably, proved far more troublesome. With all its nooks and crannies—any of which were large enough to contain a single ring—I managed to open only a few drawers and cabinets before taking a step back and reviewing my options.

After a moment's consideration, I decided that if the Aesir *had* left the ring here it would be in one of two places: somewhere obvious but nearly impossible to access, or somewhere so clever I'd have trouble locating it even if I had all the time in the world.

And so, with that in mind, I gave up my search of the kitchen and returned instead to the locked chest.

I dropped to my knees in front of it, inspecting the padlock. It was cast iron by the look of it, the sort that featured in old pirate movies. It was an oddly clumsy, clunky thing; with the right tools, I'd have been able to pick it in no time flat. Unfortunately, I didn't have the right tools.

I did, however, have a hammer.

Once I had the tool firmly in hand, I angled myself so that—when I struck—I brought the ball end down on the side with the fixed end of the shackle, then pried at the shackle loop to create tension. It took several strikes, each seeming somehow noisier than the last, but eventually the pins disengaged and the lock popped open.

"And they said I'd never amount to anythin'," I muttered gleefully. "Take *that*, Mr. Tushman. I told ye I'd do great t'ings, someday, didn't I? Ye twat waffle."

I twisted the padlock, removed it, and threw back the lid of the chest...only to find an even smaller chest inside, this one also locked.

"Oh, ye motherfucker..."

In the end, I repeated this laborious process three more times with each new chest emerging smaller than the last until at last I held a container no larger than a jewelry box. This lock I was able to shatter with a single blow of my hammer, though I admit I may have swung it a few more times out of frustration.

And by a few I mean a dozen more times.

"Of course," I grumbled as I stared down at the box. Or, should I say, what little remained of it; the container lay in pieces, its velveteen interior scratched and torn, its contents predictably empty.

"Looking for this?"

I jumped, so startled by the sudden and unexpected interruption that my heart was pounding in my ears, and whirled to point an accusatory finger at the speaker.

"Okay, seriously, how *the fuck* d'ye keep doin' that?!" I demanded. "I mean it. This is like the third time in three days!"

Vé's look was eloquent as he brandished the precious ring I'd worked so hard to find between his thumb and forefinger. "Magic, of course. Isn't it obvious?"

CHAPTER 33

I didn't bother going for the door. I knew I'd never make it past one of the Aesir. Certainly not as limited as I was, now. Instead, I flung my hammer at the son of a bitch's face and made a break for the next room over. If I could just make it to the hallway, I knew I stood at least a chance of rejoining Hilde and getting away—assuming the Valkyrie remained at her post.

Unfortunately, I'd only managed a few steps into the room when a heavy object of some sort crashed into me from behind. One of the wicker chairs, maybe? Either way, I went sprawling immediately and ended up draped halfway over the coffee table. I groaned and tried to stand back up, but someone grabbed me about the waist and body slammed me to the floor.

"Don't make me pin you a second time," a woman's voice growled as she twisted my arm up and behind my back.

I screamed from the sudden pain.

"Now, now, Gerde," Vé said, padding into the room like a cat, careful to avoid my thrashing legs as he sidled into view. "There's no need for idle threats. We wouldn't want our friend here to get the wrong impression."

"And what impression would that be?" I asked through gritted teeth.

"Why, that you have even the slightest chance of getting away, of course."

While he may have been a two-faced son of a giantess, I quickly discovered Vé was a god of his word; within a matter of minutes, he and Gerde had me tied up on the bed. And not in a sexy way, either. They'd bound my hands and feet together with a single bed sheet so that I had no choice but to lay on my side and stare at an utterly bland and uninteresting patch of wall.

"Must we do this all day?" Vé was saying. "Simply tell me who sent you, and this can all be over. While I appreciate your high tolerance for pain, and I truly do, the fact is I can wait here as long as it takes. In the meantime, I expect your poor mortal limbs have already started cramping."

Vé was right. My legs were aching so badly I wanted to cry. My back and shoulders, too. And yet, still I refused to tell them anything more than I had when they'd first thrown me onto the bed—which was nothing.

"She isn't going to talk to us," Gerde said, correctly anticipating my thoughts. "She won't betray whoever she's working for."

"Oh, I already know who she's working for," Vé replied.

"You do? Who is it?"

"My eldest brother."

I blinked, trying to keep my surprise hidden and my expression neutral. Did he really think Odin was pulling my strings? But why?

"The Allfather?!" Gerde exclaimed. "But he would never stoop to something like this. Or work with someone like *her*."

"You don't think so? And what about earlier today, when you tried to convince Freya that this mortal was a spy?"

"Sure, but not for Odin."

"Ah, but what happened when you told her?"

"She wouldn't listen to me."

"She wouldn't listen to you! And why is that? Because she doesn't trust you? Or is it because she already knew this creature was a spy?"

"I don't—"

"You were the one who told me that Freya and this woman have crossed paths," Vé went on, relentlessly. "You were the one who said she'd been to Fólkvangr before. And yet you claim you found her in Valhalla? In my eldest brother's chosen realm? If that's true, then how can you be so sure she *isn't* working for him?"

"I...I don't know."

For a moment, I could hardly believe my ears. It had been *Gerde* who outed me to Vé? And all because she'd been suspicious of me? It made a twisted sort of sense, I supposed; I had sort of appeared out of thin air at a particularly inopportune time. Still, to go to one of Odin's rivals with that information?

And yet, based on the tone of their conversation, it didn't sound as though Gerde was working for Vé, directly. Indeed, it seemed as though I had to at least consider the possibility that she, too, was being manipulated. Perhaps she was no different than Sif had been in that regard—a pawn who'd believed herself a queen.

A pawn who needed her ass beat, but still.

Unfortunately, knowing all that wasn't going to do me a lick of good. Whatever pleas I might have made to Gerde's sense of reason were bound to be misconstrued, at best. Plus, I couldn't risk saying something I shouldn't and giving Vé what he so clearly wanted: a target.

"Well I'm telling you, she won't talk," Gerde said, eventually, her voice troubled. "So what do you want to do with her?"

"Do with her?"

"Yes. Shouldn't we turn her in?"

"And give Odin the chance to set her free? No. No, I think I will leave her here, for now. The Folkmoot is due to begin shortly. I can decide what I want to do with her, afterwards."

"What if she—"

"You go on ahead," Vé cut in. "I wish to have a word with the thief in private. And tell the guards outside that have just arrived to go. They won't be needed."

Gerde must have hesitated, because when Vé spoke again it was with far less warmth.

"I said go."

I heard the door open and slam shut.

Vé sighed. "Finally. I thought she'd never leave." His weight settled onto the mattress beside me, causing it to bounce and jiggle. "My elder brother was correct before, you know. I truly do enjoy a bit of theater. I always have. But that does not mean I relish having to perform every waking hour of every day. It can get so tiring. And keeping all the lies straight in one's head! Sometimes it's nice to have someone to talk to. Someone you can be honest with. Do you know what I mean?"

I must have made some sound, perhaps a wince of pain, because the Aesir went on as though I'd agreed with him.

"Oh, good! I feel like a weight's been lifted off my shoulders, you have no idea. You see, ordinarily I'd have to lie and pat your head and assure you that I meant no harm. I would never *ever* tell you, for example, that you were going to die, or that I planned to make it look as though your friend outside, the lovely Valkyrie I knocked unconscious on my way in, did the deed. And of course I'd never confess that she was doomed to die as well. But now I feel like I can! It's so...liberating."

After listening to his entire rant and learning what the demented god intended to do, I began thrashing violently against my restraints, trying desperately to get free. I even attempted to scream for help, though the bastard's hand clamped down on my mouth almost immediately.

"Now, now. None of that. Remember, you said I could be brutally honest with you. Besides, we wouldn't want to have to involve anyone else, now would we? After all, more corpses would only lead to more questions. No. It's much better to keep it simple. This way I can claim the Allfather sent you to kill me, and perhaps would have succeeded if not for the noble sacrifice of your Valkyrie friend. That should be enough to make me seem like a legitimate threat to his rule, not to mention discredit his claim to the throne, don't you think?"

I tried to say something despite his hand.

"Hmm? What was that? Oh, yes. Gerde. I'll have to take care of her as well, of course. But there'll be time for that later. She's not the type to assume the worst of any of *us*. Besides, I could always claim I left you here alive and that the Valkyrie fought you for her own reasons. That is the thing about lies, my dear...they are often far easier to stomach than the truth."

I sagged as Vé finished his little monologue, realizing too late that the Aesir had somehow thought of everything. Not that it was a perfect murder plot; it wasn't. There were enough holes in it that others, like Róta and Freya for instance, would eventually piece together what had actually happened. But it wasn't as though anyone would willingly take their word for it over his—especially not if it meant implicating themselves in the process.

"Well then," Vé said with an air of bustling efficiency, "that's enough chit chat for one afternoon. Let's get on with your murder, shall we?"

CHAPTER 34

I would have liked to say that I sprang free when Vé untied me, but that simply wasn't the case. Instead, I whimpered and groaned, my limbs stiff and aching from being pinned behind me for so long—the resumption of blood flow like the persistent sting of bees up my arms and legs. The longer this went on, the more I cursed my own weakness. Not so long ago, I could have broken free of my restraints with nothing but brute strength alone, not to mention turned the table on my captors. But now here I was, an ordinary woman with modest abilities and mediocre people skills.

In other words: the perfect victim.

"There, there," Vé said as he picked me up off the bed in a fireman's carry, ignoring my feeble attempts to fend him off. "Don't you worry. Soon you won't feel a thing. Won't that be nice? Now, let's see... should you die by the door over here? Or in the main room? I think maybe the main room. The overturned furniture in there will really add to the ambience. Everyone loves a messy crime scene."

I tucked my head into the Aesir's chest as if to hide my tear-stained face. In truth, it was to hide my mounting disgust. What kind of monster was he to talk so casually about murder, especially in front of the person he intended to kill? And pinning the murder on

Hilde...it took a cold, ruthless individual to consider such things. A true psychopath.

Of course, he wasn't the first of his kind I'd ever met.

Nor would he be the last.

As Vé started walking, I muttered something into the folds of his tunic, so softly that there was no way the Aesir would have heard me.

"What was that? Speak up, my dear. It'd be a tragedy for no one to hear your final words."

I repeated myself, albeit just as softly.

Vé made an exasperated sound and held me out from his body like one might a child, his otherworldly strength so great that his arms barely quivered from the effort.

"What are you babbling about?" he demanded.

I let my eyes wander across the god's ridiculously handsome face and down the length of his comely neck and chiseled chest, all too aware of how very cruel it was that something so perfectly proportioned could hide such a twisted personality.

I cleared my suddenly dry, raspy throat. "What I said was...all I want for Christmas...is ye..."

"Oh! Well, that's nice. I'm afraid you'll still have to die, but I appreciate—"

"In a body bag."

As soon as the words left my mouth, I shot my previously dangling arm up and dealt a savage blow to the Aesir's unprotected throat. He dropped me instantly, clutching at a wound from which golden ichor had already begun to spray. I landed hard—so hard in fact that the shard of Bifrosted glass I'd used to wound the immortal shattered into a dozen pieces beneath my weight.

I scampered backwards, avoiding the Aesir's clumsy attempt to swipe at me. Already his blood had begun to soak his clothes and puddle on the floor, dousing all it touched with what looked eerily like metallic paint. Panicked lest he recover and come after me, I spun and leapt to my feet, forced to leave the remnants of the rainbow glass behind as I fled.

Vé tried to yell, then, but I must have caught his larynx because all he managed was a gurgle filled with pent up rage.

Once I'd made it to the hallway and slammed the door shut behind me, I went to look for Hilde. Finding her didn't take long; the Valkyrie lay slumped against the wall where I'd left her, blood trickling down her face from a wound on her scalp, her bangs matted with the stuff. I bent down and shook her.

"Hilde! Hilde get up. We have to go."

The Valkyrie groaned but didn't wake.

So, with no time to waste and a psychopath to avoid, I did what everyone suggests you do when you see someone with a possible concussion: I slapped her across the face. Hard.

"Wake up!"

A hand clamped tight around my throat and squeezed so tightly it felt like my eyes might explode right out of my head. I reached for the wrist it was attached to and tapped it several times to indicate my submission.

Hilde relaxed her grip. "Don't you ever...ever...do that again. Are we clear?"

"Totally," I rasped.

"Now...why am I on the floor?"

"First, let's get you up. We can't afford to stay here." I dragged Hilde to her feet and together we shuffled down the corridor. As we walked, I explained as concisely as I could how we'd ended up fleeing down a hallway together, leaving out nothing but the most minor details.

"I can't believe that bastard meant to kill us," Hilde said when I'd finished. "And you said you stabbed him?"

"With the Bifrosted glass. It was the only t'ing I could t'ink of that might hurt him. Luckily, it worked. I still don't know how Gerde managed to miss it when she tied me up."

"Gerde, too." Hilde let out a pained sigh. "I knew she was upset, but I never thought she'd go that far."

"Aye. Though I doubt she t'inks she's done anythin' wrong. I imagine we look like the bad guys, from her perspective."

Hilde arched an eyebrow.

"What? I'm not defendin' her or anythin'. Just sayin' it might've been better if we'd just told the truth from the beginnin'."

"Yeah, you might be right about that. But it's too late now to cry over spilled beer. So, what's next? Obviously we have to get you far away from here. It's way too risky to stick around with one of the Aesir out for your blood. Especially considering how willing he was to kill you *before* you slit his throat. I honestly think our best bet is to steal one of the sleighs and—"

"No," I interjected, firmly. "I'm not runnin' away. Besides, I told ye already, I won't leave here until ye can come with me."

Hilde shook her head. "Forget about that. Look, we know now how far Vé is willing to go to take the throne, but we still don't have any proof. Even if we could convince Gerde or Sif to talk, it wouldn't be enough to guarantee he'll be found guilty, which is the only thing that could keep you safe from him."

"And who said we don't have any proof?"

"What—"

I grinned maniacally as I held up the ring I'd managed to lift from Vé's coin purse when he'd lifted me off the bed. "Come on. I used to make a livin' stealin' t'ings like this. Give me some credit."

"As an officer of the law, I'm going to pretend I didn't hear that. But, as your friend..." Hilde snatched me up in a bear hug that caught me so by surprise I very nearly fumbled the ring.

"T'anks," I said, chuckling.

Hilde drew back, her unguarded smile transforming her icy beauty into something warm and inviting—an expression I'd seen on her face before, but never aimed at me. "So, what do you want to do?" she asked.

"Storm the Folkmoot and expose Vé for the monster that he is."

"I should have known." Hilde smirked and slapped me on the shoulder. "Alright, then. Follow me. I know the way."

CHAPTER 35

Once Hilde was feeling recovered enough to manage a quicker pace, we ran—careening down corridors and sprinting up whole flights of stairs until, at last, we reached the great hall's foyer. Here we stopped to catch our breath, take stock of our surroundings, and ultimately curse a fickle and unforgiving universe.

The doors were locked.

"Ye have got to be kiddin' me!"

"Yeah, that's not good."

I approached the immense, interwoven branches that formed the lock and tried to wrench them apart, but it was no use; most of the limbs were as thick as my own. Besides, it wouldn't be much of a lock if breaking it was something an ordinary person could pull off. The question was, why was it shut?

"D'ye t'ink they could've started the Folkmoot already?" I asked, kicking at the base of the door in frustration.

"It's possible."

I had a thought. "Wait, what about Vé? Wouldn't they have waited for him before lockin' the doors?"

"I don't know. Maybe there weren't any speeches scheduled today? Or maybe..."

"Or maybe he beat us here somehow and is already in there tellin' everyone that we tried to kill him," I supplied, speaking aloud the insidious thought that had clearly just occurred to both of us.

"Yeah. Or that."

"Oh, well," I said with a heavy sigh. "I guess that's a risk we'll have to take. Come on, we can still use the side entrance. Ye remember the way, don't ye?"

"I do, but we can't."

"What? Why?"

"Because there are einherjar guarding it, now. Odin's orders. He saw where you emerged from yesterday and didn't want another interruption, so he's stationed some of his men outside the service corridor. They'd never let us through without a fight, and I doubt we'd be able to take them on our own. Not unless we were willing to really hurt them."

"Which we're not?" I ventured.

"Which we're not."

"Okay, fine. So what do ye suggest?"

Rather than reply, Hilde turned on her heel and marched over to an installation displayed on a nearby wall—a pair of battle axes crossed over a studded leather targe. With a snarl, she tore both weapons free and tossed one to me. A quick inspection of the blade revealed a shockingly sharp edge.

I hefted the haft of the axe to rest on my shoulder. "Ye lot do understand what 'just for decoration' means, don't ye?"

Hilde snorted indelicately. "What's the point of something pretty if it can't hurt you?"

"Such a barbarian," I teased.

"And proud of it. Now, come on. This door won't chop itself down."

CHAPTER 36

Before you ask, no, the two of us did not manage to chop down the doors to the great hall. We did, however, manage to annoy those inside enough with our incessant banging and unorthodox battle cries that they decided to open them for us.

"This one's for making us wait years for your next book!" I bellowed as I drew back to deliver yet another strike. "You lazy, inconsiderate bastards!"

"Hold on." Hilde shot out an arm to halt me. "It's opening."

I paused to watch the branches as they began to shrink and unravel, sinking back into the doors like tree roots growing in reverse. Moments later, a heavy thunk sounded and the doors began to swing open at a glacial pace. I peered through that gap and saw at least two others doing the same—presumably those tasked with guarding the entrance.

Relieved and more exhausted than I cared to admit, I tossed my battle axe to Hilde. "Ye remember the plan?"

The Valkyrie nodded. "Get a sleigh ready just in case it's a trap. Though I'm still not sure why you're the one who's going in instead of me."

"Because ye work for Freya, whereas I can honestly say I don't. In fact, I will say it. They need to hear the truth from someone impartial. Besides, I don't know the first t'ing about the tower's layout. I'd just end up runnin' around in circles."

"Okay, fine. But what happens if they capture you?"

"Then I'll have to escape and meet ye down there. Or, if I can't, you'll have to find Róta and break me out. Either way, there's no sense in both of us gettin' caught."

"I don't like it, but I guess we don't have a choice. You have to promise me you'll be careful, alright?"

"I'd rather be lucky," I replied with a wink. Then, before I could overthink how colossally risky it was to do so, I bolted through the slender opening, determined to make it past the guards. This I managed, though it was more a matter of chance than anything; the nearest guard was too busy tugging on the absurdly heavy door to stop me rushing past.

The instant I reached the middle of the room, however, I found myself surrounded by spear tips and naked steel blades held by both Valkyries and einherjar. I raised both hands in surrender, making it clear I wasn't a threat, but it didn't matter; the great hall was suddenly filled with angry shouts and disbelieving jeers, saying things like "her again?!" and "what's she doing here?!"

Until, that is, a thunderous crash silenced them all.

Odin, towering over us all in a scarlet cloak with a fur collar that swallowed his shoulders whole and a horned helmet that added at least a foot to his height, raised the wizened staff he'd beat against the floor and leveled it at me as though it were a loaded gun. "How dare you try to break in here?"

"Husband, perhaps we should—" began Freya, who stood at the Allfather's side in a gown that looked to have been made of liquid silver.

"No! She has interrupted us for the last time. Get her out of my sight!"

The nearby Valkyries stayed where they were, clearly unwilling to make a move without Freya's permission. And so it ended up being one of the einherjar who stepped forward to grab my arm and haul me off. Unfortunately for him, I wasn't about to let that happen.

Not again. Not ever.

As the warrior's grubby fingers closed over my right wrist, I twisted and drove the elbow of that same arm into the poor sucker's face. The einherjar's head snapped back and he stumbled backwards bleeding from a shattered nose.

"I have proof!" I shouted, holding up the ring I'd stolen from Vé. "Proof of what Lord Vé has done!"

I wasn't sure what I expected to happen. Perhaps I hoped the words would be enough—that the scene would play out like every signature moment from every great movie in which good triumphs over evil. The instant we see Sarah Connor staring at a mangled machine arm. The moment Westley stands on his own two feet to face Humperdinck. The heart-stopping climax when Neo pulls a bullet out of thin air.

Spoiler alert: it didn't.

Instead, it turned out Odin was far too incensed to listen; he bellowed a command and four more of his men came at me, grabbing a limb apiece and holding me in place like a sacrificial lamb for the slaughter. I writhed and wriggled, desperate to get free and reveal the truth, but there was simply nothing I could do.

"Hold!"

The call came from one of the Valkyries guarding the crowd, and I felt a momentary flicker of hope. At least until I saw the Valkyrie in question step forward in her skimpy armor, at which point all my aspirations were reduced to ash.

"Gerde, I—"

The Valkyrie ignored me completely and instead snatched at the hand holding Draupnir. I tried to yank it from her, but she was too strong; she managed to wrench open my fingers and pry the ring from my grasp.

"Stop! That's evidence! Ye can't—"

"That's enough!" Odin shouted, his voice roaring through the room like a torrential gust of wind, causing banners to whip about and place settings to fly. "Take her away! I will deal with her person-ally, later."

I watched in horror as Freya, her eyes brimming with unshed tears, tried to reason with her husband. But I knew it was no use; the Allfather's mind was made up, and nothing I said or did would change that. Besides, my proof was now in the hands of someone who not only didn't trust me, but thought me a thief and a spy.

The einherjar started to carry me off, and I had just begun to think things couldn't possibly get any worse when I saw Vé enter the great hall. Though he'd changed clothes since I'd last seen him, the Aesir appeared healthy and whole, his throat unblemished. Worse still, he was smiling, grinning at me like a loan shark who knew he had me by my jingle bells. He even went so far as to blow me a kiss. And that's when I knew.

It was all over.

And I was as good as dead.

CHAPTER 37

"**S**top!"

If Odin's voice had lashed at us all like a gust of wind, this one struck us all between the eyes like a hammer. Indeed, the einherjar who held me aloft sagged beneath its weight, very nearly dropping me on the threshold in the process. As they struggled to recover, I craned my neck to see who'd spoken and found a familiar, one-handed figure approaching the dais upon which Odin and Freya stood.

Tyr.

The Aesir halted at the foot of the dais. "I believe we should hear what the mortal has to say, Allfather."

I prepared myself for Odin's reply, all too aware that he was unlikely to see reason this late in the game. And yet, miraculously, the Allfather seemed to calm down. Indeed, his expression was thoughtful as he regarded his fellow Asgardian. "Do you wish to hear her testimony as a member of the Hird? Or as her judge?"

"Her judge."

The Hird gasped collectively at this, though I couldn't for the life of me figure out why. At best, I guessed it had something to do with Tyr's status, or perhaps his righteous sense of justice. What I did know, however, was how incensed Vé was by the pronouncement; he strutted past me and marched right up to the dais to jab an accusatory finger in Odin's face.

"You cannot allow this!" he snarled.

"Is that so?"

Something in Odin's tone must have warned Vé, because he immediately turned his attention instead to the crowds at their tables. "What I mean to say is that this mortal has disrespected not only you, Allfather, but everyone here with her flagrant disregard for our ways! To hear her out now would be no different than allowing a disease riddled animal to wander in and shit on our floors."

"Perhaps," Odin replied, his expression guarded. "However, Tyr is the one who wishes to hear her speak, not I. And I need not remind you that it is Tyr's right to ask this of me, just as it was your right to call a Folkmoot. Or would you rather I ignore his request according to my whim, alone? Tell me, little brother, is that how you would lead our people?"

"No, of course not," Vé replied smoothly as discontented murmurs began to sound from the crowd.

"Then I shall allow Tyr to proceed. Unless you have some other reason for not wishing to hear the woman speak that you have not told us?"

Vé pursed his lips. "None whatsoever."

"Very well, then. Einherjar! Bring the mortal here so that all may hear what she has to say."

The men holding me did as they were instructed at once, effectively parading me in front of the entire assembly in the process. Personally, I would have been far happier to walk on my own two feet, but I wasn't about to rock the palanquin. Not if I could help it.

At last, the einherjar set me down in front of the dais. I wobbled a little as my feet touched the ground, and one of the men reached out to steady me. I swatted his hand away.

"Touch me again and I swear I'll roast your chestnuts over an open fire," I hissed.

"Enough," Odin said, rapping his staff on the floor for the second time. "You may return to your posts."

As the einherjar wandered off, Tyr stepped forward to loom over me. He looked grim, nothing at all like he had when we'd exchanged idle banter over a few flagons of mead the day before. But, when he bid me to speak with a wave of his good arm, I swore I saw a glimmer of anticipation in his eyes.

And so speak I did.

"Lords and ladies of the Hird!" I began. "Ye may not know me, though I have no doubt ye remember me from yesterday. For that I must apologize. I did not intend to interrupt your meal then, and I regret havin' to, now. However, I had no choice. You see, yesterday I discovered that Lord Vé here had a spy in Lord Vili's camp, a spy whose conscience pricked them to confess that the ring given to Lord Vili was not in fact Draupnir, but Andvari's Gift in disguise."

I searched for Vili's face in the crowd and found it filled with both doubt and anger, though which of the emotions were reserved for me, I couldn't be sure.

"Moreover," I continued, "this spy told me that Lord Vé knew of this deception. That in fact it was his idea to use it as a means to implicate Nate Temple in his brother's very likely death."

"Now wait a minute—" Vé began.

"You will have your turn to speak in your defense," Tyr cut in. "Until then, you will be silent."

"Ye see," I went on, undeterred, "it was Lord Vé's intention to both remove his competition and bind ye together against a common enemy. It was, in fact, the same logic he applied when he attempted to kill me and one of Lady Freya's Valkyries not but an hour ago in the hopes of underminin' the Allfather's authority."

"And how would that undermine the Allfather?" Tyr asked.

"Lord Vé believed, or at least claimed he believed, I worked for the Allfather."

"But you do not?"

"No," I replied, fervently. "I don't work for anyone. Not the Allfather, not Lady Freya. I am not an aspirin' Valkyrie. I'm a refugee who Lady Freya wanted to shelter and protect."

"I see." Tyr folded his arms across his expansive chest. "And what proof do you have to substantiate your claims?"

"I...none, I'm afraid," I confessed. I quickly scanned the crowd but saw no sign of Gerde amongst the gathered faces and had to assume she'd left with the ring. "Only me word. I did have somethin' more concrete when I arrived, but it was taken from me right before I was escorted out."

"Escorted." Vé snorted, his eyes twinkling with malice and triumph. "You were being thrown out! And now you tell this ridiculous lie and expect us to believe the proof was stolen from you? How foolish do you think we are?"

If Tyr minded this sudden outburst, it didn't show. Instead, he inclined his head. "It is customary to provide evidence to back such claims," he confirmed. "Without it, and with no one to corroborate your tale, I cannot pass judgment."

I felt my shoulders sag. It was hopeless. Tyr was right; I had no way to prove Vé had done what I'd accused him of. If anything, the more I protested his guilt, the more indignant he'd be allowed to act. What I needed, I realized, was to provoke Vé into a confession—or at least sow a seed of doubt in everyone's minds. Especially Vili's. After all, if I could get him on my side...

"Wait!" I urged. "I *can* prove it!"

A flicker of a smile graced Tyr's lips—so fleeting I wondered if I'd imagined it. "Then do."

"May I ask for someone to join us?"

"If you must."

"Oh, for all the...how long are we going to let this farce continue?!" Vé demanded, throwing his arms wide in exasperation.

"Until I am satisfied," was Tyr's reply. "Why? Do you have a problem with that?"

Vé sighed and raised both hands in mock surrender. "Of course not. It has always been your right to sit in judgment of us, and no one would ever presume to tell you how to do your job. Although...if you cannot tell as the rest of us can that this mortal is *clearly* lying through her rotting teeth, perhaps you should consider retirement."

Tyr met the gaze of his fellow Aesir in total silence.

"Just a suggestion," Vé added, slyly.

Tyr turned to me. "Who do you wish to join us?"

I told him.

"Very well," Tyr said. "Vili, please join us!"

The second son rose haughtily from his seat and took the long route to reach us—clearly basking in the sudden attention. I stole a quick glance at his younger brother's bemused face, confirming from it that he had no idea what I was planning.

Good.

"Lord Vili," I began once the god in question arrived, "I appreciate your assistance."

"I am not here to assist you, mortal," Vili replied, his voice far louder than it needed to be. "I am here because Tyr asked for me, and because I believe in our justice system."

"Spoken like a true politician," I muttered.

"What was that?"

"Nothin'. Look, as long as ye answer me questions honestly, I don't really care what your reasons are, alright? Now, can I trust ye to do that?"

"Of course," he replied, stiffly.

"Excellent. Lord Vili...is it true that Lord Vé gave ye a gift yesterday?"

"It is."

"And what was that gift?"

Vili rolled his eyes. "I believe you've already been over this. It was Draupnir."

"And who did he say the gift was from?"

"He...well, from him."

"Courtesy of Nate Temple though, yes?"

"Yes. But that doesn't—"

"And d'ye have it on your person, now?" I asked.

The Aesir pressed a hand to his chest. "Why do you need to know that?"

"It's a simple question. D'ye have it?"

"I do."

"And have ye tried it on, yet?"

"I have not."

I felt more than saw Vé stiffen beside me, but it was already too late; I had him right where I wanted him. I turned to Tyr. "To prove whether me claim is true or false, I would like Lord Vé to put on the ring he gave to Lord Vili."

"Of all the ridiculous—" Vé began.

"*If* everythin' I've said is a lie," I interjected, cutting off Vé's vitriolic response before he could generate any momentum, "Lord Vé should have no fear whatsoever of puttin' on the ring. If, however, what I say is true, doin' so is sure to kill him."

"Hmm. I suppose that would be a simple solution." Tyr turned to Vé in anticipation. "Well, what say you?"

"Absolutely not! I refuse to accept this deranged creature's notion of compromise. After all, how am I to know this was not some plot concocted by my brother, Vili? Perhaps the ring *is* cursed. A curse he himself put on it and has cleverly arranged to see placed on my finger!"

"You would accuse me?!" Vili bellowed indignantly, his cheeks purpling with rage.

"I do not accuse anyone. I am merely being practical. Perhaps you had nothing to do with it, and this is all some elaborate trap set up by the two who stand to gain the most from our conflict." Vé swung his gaze upon Odin and Freya. "It would not be the first time these two manipulated us to their own ends. In fact—"

"Liar!"

The shout brought all of us around to stare at the woman who strode into the center of the room. There, her chest rising and falling dramatically, her arm practically vibrating with anger, stood Gerde with her hand held out. In her palm sat the ring she'd taken from me.

"Quinn is telling the truth!" she cried. "It is Lord Vé who lies! I took this from her, and I believe now it is the real Draupnir! Which means the ring he has given his brother *will* kill him, and that's why he refuses to wear it."

Next to me, I heard Vé stifle a curse.

"Is this true?!" Vili shouted, wheeling on his sibling.

Only Vé wasn't there.

And that's when all hell broke loose.

CHAPTER 38

The great hall erupted as someone or something shoved Vili into me, sending the two of us tumbling to the ground in a tangle of limbs. After extricating myself, I saw Odin's einherjar and Freya's Valkyries fan out to keep the outraged members of the Hird from mobbing us. Of Vé, I saw no sign at all.

"He's used an illusion to make himself invisible," Vili said, sitting up and gesturing towards the exit. "He'll be going for the door! Someone stop him!"

But no one could hear him above the sounds of an increasingly animated crowd. I rose to my feet, preparing to race after the Aesir myself when I heard a scream of pain. And that's when I noticed Gerde crumpled on the floor clutching at a vicious looking wound on her arm.

She saw me looking and pointed with a bloodsoaked hand. "He took the ring!"

I took off immediately, sprinting past the injured Valkyrie and heading straight for the door—not that I knew what I'd do when I caught up to the bastard. After all, I'd been incredibly fortunate to wound him before, and even that hadn't exactly proven fatal. Plus, he was invisible. What if he doubled back and took me as his hostage, or simply waited until I passed and stabbed me from behind?

Realizing how foolish such a blind pursuit might prove, I started to second guess my decision. But then I saw one of the einherjar near the door get knocked off his feet as if by some unseen force and knew that Vé was just up ahead—as did several of the einherjar's companions, who must have noticed the same thing and decided to give chase.

Resolved to join them, I ran harder, my arms pumping so quickly my legs had no choice but to keep up. I was sprinting so fast, in fact, that I only just managed to skid to a halt before I barreled directly into the wall of motionless einherjar crowding the gaping doorway.

"Oy! What the hell are ye doin'? Get out there and catch him!" When none of them answered me, I groaned and shoved myself into their midst, forcing them to step aside until at last I managed to reach the foyer.

Where I found Heimdall, standing over Vé's prostrated body holding a cracked mug from which dribbled a heady mixture of golden ichor and Yuletide Punch.

"Oh, hello," he said, hoisting his drink in a salute before quaffing its contents and finishing with a lusty sigh. "I really do love this time of year. Don't you?"

CHAPTER 39

Once everyone was finally settled down, Gerde's injury had been seen to by the lovely Eir, and the unconscious Vé was properly restrained, Tyr addressed the assembly in its entirety while the Allfather looked on. Despite the mania of the past hour or so, I noticed the one-eyed bastard seemed rather pleased with the situation—almost as if he'd planned for this outcome all along. Not that I could see how.

I shook my head and turned my attention back to the one-handed Aesir, who was busy restating the facts of the case against Vé as they'd been presented to him, including both the allegations as well as the proof that supported them, before delivering his verdict.

"I find Vé, third son of Borr and brother of Odin, guilty," he intoned. "Of all charges."

For once, no one spoke.

Odin slammed the end of his staff on the ground once, then again. "You have heard Tyr's ruling, and it is a ruling we must all respect. As for Vé's punishment, that will be decided at a later date. For now, he will be taken away, confined to a cell, and his magic sealed."

But I was having none of that.

"That's not good enough!" I shouted.

Odin, no doubt unused to being interrupted, turned to me with a rebuke fresh on his lips.

"No," I snapped. "I won't have ye talkin' down like that to me again. I don't work for ye. And I don't work for your wife, either. I came here lookin' for help, and instead I nearly got killed *under your watch*! And *still* I put me life on the line to expose this bastard. Now I t'ink that should earn me a little respect, don't ye?"

Odin pursed his lips. "Perhaps."

"It does," Freya interjected, putting a hand on her husband's shoulder and squeezing rather harder than necessary. "And we are grateful. Aren't we, dear?"

"Yes, fine," Odin grumbled. "We're grateful."

"Then tell me this...are ye plannin' to execute the son of a bitch?"

Odin arched a single eyebrow. "You do realize he and I shared the same womb."

I winced. "Okay, maybe not the best choice of words. But ye know what I'm askin'."

Odin sighed. "I do. And I cannot promise he'll face so definitive a punishment as death. But I *can* promise you that, when we are done with him, he'll wish he had."

I shook my head, knowing in my heart of hearts that it wasn't enough. And yet, as I studied the faces around me, I realized that it was the best I could expect. I doubted even Tyr, who personified justice, could condone snuffing out a candle that was meant to burn until the end of time. So, rather than argue, I decided to be charitable.

'Twas the season, after all.

"I'll hold ye to that."

"I'd expect nothing less. Now—"

The rest of what the Allfather intended to say was lost as the window behind him exploded in a shower of glass.

CHAPTER 40

The sleigh that crashed through the window of the great hall soared over our heads and landed with a tremendous clatter before skidding halfway across the room, colliding with a table, and scattering its terrified occupants. I noticed Hilde at the reins at once, her face paler even than it usually was, though this time the reins were taut and attached to something.

Two somethings, actually.

"Whoo! Check us out! We totally rammed that motherfucking window!"

"You're fucking right we did! It was like 'ooh look at me I'm all transparent and shit' and we were like 'yippee ki yay you lil' bitch'!"

"That's what I'm talking about!"

"Roll YULETIDE!"

The two foul-mouthed individuals—who just so happened to be a pair of knobby-kneed, long-faced goats—turned and bashed their horned heads together the way fraternity bros might bump chests.

"I thought you sent them away!" I heard Freya say to her husband in a low hiss.

Odin sighed. "I did."

"Hey!" cried one of the goats. "Look who it is! It's the Eyefather!"

"Oh yeah! If it isn't Captain Rehab! Careful, or you'll tear your eye out!"

"Too late!" brayed his companion.

"Enough!" Odin commanded in his sternest voice. But the goats kept right on chattering, and eventually the Allfather had no choice but to ignore them in favor of addressing Hilde, who'd abandoned the sleigh and joined me at the foot of the dais.

"Explain," was all he said.

Hilde shot me a nervous look and cleared her throat. "Ah, yes, Allfather. Well, you see, I went to requisition one of the sleighs, but it seemed they'd all been decommissioned except that one."

"And what did you need the sleigh for?"

"Um..."

"To rescue me," I interjected. "In case Vé got away with it. Hilde is me friend. The Valkyrie I mentioned in me testimony."

"Hilde? Brunhilde's daughter?" Odin's eye widened. "I thought you'd gone missing."

"It's a long story," Hilde replied, cagily. "But what Quinn says is true. I convinced Tanngrisnir and Tanngnjóstr to pull the sleigh, but when I told them to fly past the window so I could see what was happening in the great hall, they...well..."

We all turned to look at the remains of the window, then to the two goats.

"They're looking at us again," noted the darker of the two.

"It's because they want to eat us."

"Oh yeah? You want to eat us? Huh?! Come on, then! Come and get you some!"

"Yeah, come and eat my asshole, you ho-ho-whores!"

I shook my head and swung back around to stare up at Odin. "What the fuck is wrong with those two?"

"They belonged to my son, Thor. He used to make them pull his sleigh, then ate them for dinner every night. Somewhere along the line, I suppose they went quite mad."

Yeah...that'd do it.

"Well," Freya interjected, "I think we've all had more than enough excitement for one day, don't you, husband? Perhaps it's time we conclude things here and begin the Yuletide celebrations. They are, after all, long overdue."

Odin let out a long sigh. "Yes, please."

And so that's what we did.

CHAPTER 41

As grim and tense as the vibe in the great hall had been when I'd first come through those enormous doors, it rapidly became twice as lively, if not downright jolly; a flagon of Yuletide Punch was pressed into every empty hand while a team of minstrels came parading down the aisles between the tables, playing festive tunes that made something jaunty out of Vé's ignominious departure. Odin ordered fuel brought and the fires stoked high to counter the gusts of wind and snow pouring in through the open window.

I left them to it, opting to avoid the festivities in favor of paying visits to those who'd helped me survive the day. First, to Gerde, who seemed well recovered enough from her injuries to endure a telling off and a well-deserved punch to the gut. I left her in Hilde's care, hoping the two might repair their fractured relationship in the aftermath of all that had happened.

Following this act of noble altruism, I went to find Tyr, who sat sipping from a modest bowl of hot stew and washing it down with mead. Beside him, Heimdall gnawed on a loaf of bread, his perfectly white teeth like an optical illusion behind his bloodless lips.

"I should've known I'd find the two of ye together," I said as I joined them. I snatched up Heimdall's unattended drink and took a quick swig. "What a day."

"I have no idea what you mean," Tyr replied, a twinkle in his eye.

"Uh huh. And I'm supposed to believe Heimdall over here was stationed just outside the door by chance, am I?"

"Who, me? Bah, I just happened to be in the right place at the right time, that's all."

"And why don't I believe ye?"

Heimdall shrugged. "Well, you know what they say. Seeing isn't believing; believing is seeing."

I rolled my eyes. "T'anks for the Christmas cookie wisdom, Bernard the Elf."

Heimdall snatched his drink back from me. "I am *not* an elf. And my name's not Bernard."

"Uh, right. Sorry."

"I'm kidding," he replied, easily. "I love that movie."

Tyr looked back and forth between Heimdall and me as though we'd lost our collective minds. "What are you two talking about?"

"Midgard stuff," Heimdall replied, winking at me. "You wouldn't understand."

"Anyway," I interjected, "I came over here to say t'anks. Genuinely. I can see now that ye were both tryin' to help in your own ways, though I do t'ink ye could've been less obtuse about it. To be honest I'm still not sure what half your vague little observations were about."

Heimdall smirked into his cup. "Give it time."

"Perhaps we could give her a hint?" Tyr suggested, nudging his companion.

"Well I suppose we *could*, it being Yuletide and all."

"Are the two of ye always like this?" I asked.

For some reason, this made them both laugh. They quickly cheersed each other and took a hearty gulp. Then, as Tyr settled back, Heimdall leaned forward—his expression deadly serious all of a sudden.

"You won't find the answers you seek here," he whispered conspiratorially. "Freya's magic is powerful, but what's been done to you is beyond her abilities."

I stiffened beneath his raptorial gaze. "And what's been done to me?"

"That is not for me to say, nor would it make sense to you if I tried. What I will tell you is that there's no point looking back. Not anymore. You have to move forward."

"I can't do that. I've lost t'ings...precious t'ings. I need 'em back. And unless I can remember where I was when they went missin', I don't see that happenin'."

"There are other ways," Heimdall replied, cryptically.

"Such as?"

"Again, I am bound by oaths too strong to answer your question directly. But I will point out that the rings you have recovered from Vé, not to mention the service you rendered by unmasking him, might offset the value of a certain suit of armor and a friend's ticket to freedom..."

I sat back, shocked both by Heimdall's unexpected knowledge and his inspired insinuation. He wasn't wrong; I could certainly make a case that whatever debts I owed the Aesir had been paid in full. In fact, it seemed entirely fair to do so in light of everything Hilde and I had risked for them.

"Ye know, I t'ink I could kiss ye right now," I confessed.

Heimdall held up a finger and sighed. "No mistletoe, I'm afraid."

"Speaking of mistletoe," Tyr chimed in helpfully, "I believe it's my turn to make a suggestion."

"I'm all ears," I told him.

"Find Loki. That should be your next step."

"Loki? What for?"

Tyr just smiled.

"Ye can't tell me either, can ye?"

"I am afraid not. If I told you, the choices you make from now on would not be your own. Better to let you weigh the scales without my tipping them, I think."

After exchanging a few more words of no particular importance, I thanked them both again and rose to my feet. They joined me, even going so far as to raise their drinks in my honor.

"To Quinn MacKenna," Tyr toasted, "the Bearer of Rings."

"And good tidings," Heimdall added, grinning. "You can't forget good tidings."

"Hear, hear!"

"Ye two are ridiculous," I insisted.

But I left smiling, all the same.

CHAPTER 42

My next stop took me back to where I'd started: at the foot of the dais. There, I encountered Freya, who rose from her throne and urged me to approach with an enthusiastic wave of her hand.

"The Allfather is busy dealing with the goats," she informed me, pointing. "They've broken into one of the mead casks and have started head-butting people."

I glanced in the direction she'd indicated just in time to see one of the Aesir get kicked in the groin by a pair of hooves as the creature they belonged to danced merrily out of Odin's fumbling reach. Punch dripped from the tuft of wiry fur beneath its chin, giving the beast a goatee of sorts—pun not intended.

"We're going bobbing for assholes!" it cried, gleefully.

Freya made a disgusted noise.

"So *that's* what all those screams were about," I said. "I thought maybe you'd gone ahead with a few public executions, or somethin'."

"No, nothing like that." Freya laughed, her smile wry as she swung her attention back to me. "You did very well, you know. Far better than I would have thought possible, under the circumstances."

I stood in silence for a moment, refusing to meet her eye lest she notice the simmering rage in my own. "Ye knew what Vé intended from the beginnin', I take it? Ye and your husband?"

Freya nodded, slowly. "We knew what he wanted; though I confess we were fools not to see how far he'd go to get it. I am sorry for what you went through. I knew as soon as he didn't show up to our meeting that he'd found out about the heist, somehow. But there was nothing I could do to warn you without arousing suspicion."

"I understand."

And I did. Unfortunately, Freya's apology rang hollow in my ears; whether she'd known how deranged her brother-in-law was or not, the fact remained she'd put me in danger with false promises and half truths.

"I know ye can't help with me memories," I told her. "And I know that ye knew it after that first session. What I don't know is why ye lied to me."

Freya looked away, guiltily. "I didn't lie. There *was* a chance I might have found another solution. But you're right. I know now that what's happened to you cannot be solved by magic. At least not mine."

"I see."

"About the armor—"

"You'll have to find it without me," I interjected. "And I expect ye to let Hilde go, just like ye promised."

Freya sighed. "Of course. That was always my intention."

"Good."

We were each of us silent for a little while after that, no doubt thinking our private thoughts. I couldn't speak to hers, but mine were focused on the memories I'd lost and how I might recover them. As for Freya and her subtle manipulations, well, I was content to let bygones be bygones.

"Oh," I said, recalling my conversation with Tyr and Heimdall. "I do have one last question. Where can I find Loki?"

"Loki? Why would you want to find him?"

"Somethin' Tyr said," I explained. "He seemed to t'ink I might find answers there."

Freya frowned. "I'm sorry, but I'm not sure where Loki is at the moment."

"Niflheim."

We turned to find Odin approaching with the decapitated heads of both goats hanging from his belt, their tongues lolling hideously from their gaping, mead-soaked mouths. He must have noticed my horror because he quickly reached down to clack their heads together.

"Hey!" the darker one bleated, his eyes refocusing instantly. "What's the big eye-dea?!"

"Yeah! What the shit, Father Dickmas?" cried the other.

"I got tired of chasing after them," Odin explained to me, ignoring the jibes that followed. "Don't worry. They'll be back to normal tomorrow."

"Unfortunately," muttered Freya.

"Anyway," Odin went on, "if you're looking for Loki, you'll find him in Niflheim. Him and Fenrir both. They've holed up in a valley there."

"You didn't tell me that," Freya said.

The Allfather shrugged. "I had Hugin and Munin follow them after we left Olympus. A precaution, that's all. I appreciate what Nate's trying to do, but he doesn't realize he's the only thing standing between us and Ragnarok. If he ends up removed from the board, even for a short time...well, let's just say his threat may not be enough to hold everyone back."

I held up a hand. "Um, d'ye mind if we get back to me for a second? Could either one of ye tell me how to get to Niflheim? Skadi guided me the last time. Oh, and a blessin' would be appreciated. Ye know, so I don't die when I get there."

"You intend to go there?" Odin asked, sounding surprised. "Why?"

"Unfinished business," I replied, cryptically.

The Allfather stroked his beard. "I'll give you my blessing, and even give you the means to travel to Loki directly, but in exchange, I want you to do something for me."

"What's that?"

He told me, and my eyes widened.

CHAPTER 43

Hilde and Róta met me in my room just as I'd finished changing back into the clothes I'd brought with me. They may not have been as practical in Fólkvangr, but they would serve me better where I was going—or at least I had to hope so. The truth was I wasn't entirely sure taking a trip to Niflheim was the right thing to do. What I did know, however, was that I wasn't satisfied with Heimdall's suggestion to accept things as they were and move on. Sure, it may have been easier, but the idea of not knowing... well, I simply couldn't live with it.

"You're sure?"

I settled a hand on Hilde's shoulder. "I am."

"And you seriously don't want me to come with you?"

"No. You've been gone long enough on me account. Though I'd appreciate it if ye could tell everyone I'm alright, and that I'll be back as soon as I can. I'd hate for 'em to worry."

"They'd worry a whole lot less if you'd just come back with me, instead," Hilde pointed out. "Niflheim is dangerous, you know."

"As is Loki," Róta added. "Not to mention Fenrir."

"Aww, I wouldn't say that. They aren't so bad once ye get to know 'em." I grinned to see Róta's shocked expression. "Aye, we met when I was in Niflheim last. Pretty sure they were in hidin' back then. Anyway, yes, I'm aware it may be dangerous. But that's why I have these."

I showed them the metal balls Odin had given me and explained their function; one would send me to Loki's camp in Niflheim, while the other would send me to an axe-throwing bar in St. Louis.

"A bar where?" Hilde asked, frowning.

"St. Louis. Apparently it was the only one he had that would send me to Midgard. But he said I should be able to find a friend there who'll help me get back to Boston, and I believe him."

Hilde nodded, looking relieved. "I'm just glad you have a way back. I'd hate to leave you stranded here."

"I know, and I appreciate it. But don't worry, I've finally got t'ings all under control. Trust me."

"Famous last words," Hilde replied, smirking.

I reached out and knocked on the wooden headboard. "There. Better?"

The Valkyrie nodded. "Just promise me you'll be careful, alright?"

"I'd rather be—"

"Lucky," she finished for me, her eyes glistening with unshed tears. "I know. But maybe do me a favor and be both, okay?"

"I'll do me best." I snatched the Valkyrie up in a brief hug, fighting back tears of my own. "Fly safe, alright? And tell Leo I said he doesn't deserve ye."

Hilde sobbed a laugh. "Consider it done."

CHAPTER 44

It'd been a long time since I'd last traveled by Gateway—or so it felt as I stepped through Odin's, trading the cozy interior of my room in Fólkvangr for the frigid, mist-drenched valleys of Niflheim. The transition left me feeling light-headed and vaguely jet lagged, as if my brain simply couldn't keep up with the sudden change.

Of course, it didn't help that the place I'd ended up in was so much dimmer than Fólkvangr with all its reflective snow and perpetual sunlight. In fact, it wasn't until the Gateway vanished that my eyes began to adjust. Fortunately, my nose and ears were working just fine, which was how I managed to track the god of mischief to his camp.

At first, all I could make out was a faint humming and the odor of smoke. Then, as I got closer, that humming became a man's voice—a lovely, if a bit tortured, tenor—singing along to the tune of Bing Crosby's "Winter Wonderland."

"Slay bells ring...are you listening? In the dark...they are whistling. A horrible sight. A terrible night. Walking into my and Fenrir's camp."

I halted and peered into the gloom, searching for the owner of the voice but finding it increasingly difficult to differentiate shapes in the roiling fog.

"Gone away...is the bluebird. Here to stay...are the buzzards. To sing a shrill song. While we right your wrong. Walking into my and Fenrir's camp."

"Hello?!" I called against my better judgment. "Is anyone out there? Loki? Fenrir?"

The singing stopped, and soon there was nothing but the sound of my own blood pulsing in my ears. I shivered, forced to rub my arms for warmth and comfort. Then, just as I was about to call out a second time, a blinding light strobed not thirty feet away—its scarlet brilliance cutting through the mist in an instant to reveal the familiar face of an absolutely monstrous, prehistoric wolf...wearing a bright red nose.

"O Holy Shite," I swore, my mouth hanging open in shock and awe.

"Don't you dare laugh," Fenrir growled in warning. "It was my father's idea."

"I, uh—"

"Doesn't he look great?" The speaker appeared as if from thin air only a few feet from his canine child, dressed head to toe in a cheap, ill-fitting costume a small town mall Santa might wear, his face all but hidden behind a bushy white beard stained pink from what I had to assume was either blood or juice, or both.

"He looks like Rudolph the Red-Nosed Paindeer," I countered.

Loki swiped lazily at the air. "Come on, he looks amazing."

"Do you want to take that off?" I asked Fenrir.

The monstrous dog nodded his shaggy head adamantly.

"Go on," I told Loki, "let him take it off."

Loki chuckled. "Fine, but you have to wear it whenever Temple comes to visit. It was a very thoughtful gift."

Fenrir growled something that might have been considered an affirmative before using his paw to fling the prosthetic to the ground, where it painted the entire clearing an eerie shade of neon red. It was then that I saw their camp in all its glory, including its fine display of holiday lights—which were in actuality copious amounts of fireflies caught in spider's webbing strung between the branches of skeletal trees.

"Charmin' place ye have here," I noted, cringing slightly. "So, d'ye still have some decoratin' to do, or..."

"I did that to keep the spies out," Loki explained. "We may have struck a truce with Odin, but that doesn't mean I want his henchbirds keeping an eye on us."

"Hugin and Munin, ye mean?"

Loki nodded, then brightened. "So, what can I do for you? And, also, who are you, again?"

"Ye don't recognize me?"

"Vaguely?" Loki waved a hand about. "I just meet so many people, you understand. It's hard to keep you all straight."

"We met in a cave. It would've been a while ago. We—"

"Oh, right! Right. The cave girl. The one who beat up Magni and Modi. Funny, you don't look the way I remember you looking."

I wasn't sure what to say to that, so instead I decided to get right down to business. "Look, I came here to ask you a few questions. But first, I made a deal with Odin to—"

A knife was suddenly at my throat as the Loki I'd been speaking to wavered and vanished in a puff of air. The real Loki, dressed the same but far more solid, leaned in so close I could smell his aftershave.

"You tell that one-eyed son of a—"

"Are ye wearin' Axe Body Spray?"

Loki hesitated. "What?"

"Ye are! Ugh, get out of here with that stuff." I shoved him back, albeit lightly—the god still had a knife.

"Why, what's wrong with how I smell?"

"Nothin', if ye wanted to smell like a homeless manchild who's too lazy to shower."

"Wow," Fenrir said, "it's like she knows you, Dad."

Loki wheeled on his son and gestured with his knife. "Children are meant to be seen and not heard! Now be quiet, the adults are talking."

Fenrir snarled.

"Sorry about that," Loki said to me. "Moody teenagers, what can you do? Anyway, where were we? Oh, right. You were about to tell me why Odin sent you before I slit your pretty throat."

"First of all, he didn't send me. He asked me to relay a message, that's all. I had me own reasons for seein' ye."

Loki frowned. "And what was the message?"

"It wasn't for ye."

Fenrir perked his head up, his ears cocked.

"Not ye, either," I said.

"Then who?"

"It's a message for Baldur."

A slow, languid smile spread across Loki's face. "Follow me."

CHAPTER 45

The god strapped to the table was one of the most physically flawless specimens I had ever seen, with a ripped physique that gym rats around the world had spent hours trying to replicate and only a few Mr. Olympia's had ever achieved. His face was equally appealing—or at least it would have been if not for the absolute terror distorting his features and the crusted snot running down his face.

"No, no, please don't do it!" he was saying as he writhed on the table, his groin covered by a skimpy pair of lime green underwear with the words "Jingle My Bells" splashed across the front in red glitter print. "Not again! I can't take it!"

I grimaced, put off by his constant whining.

"Please," he went on, turning to me in supplication, "you have to tell him to stop! I'm begging you!"

But Loki wasn't in the mood to show mercy, and I certainly wasn't in any position to stop him. The god of mischief advanced on the thrashing figure, one arm raised menacingly, his choice of weapon gleaming from the light of a nearby lamp.

"No! Oh please no!"

Loki ignored his intended victim and jabbed the base of the captive's foot, frantically working his wrist back and forth.

"NOOOOO!"

The mistletoe in Loki's hand left faint red marks where it tickled Baldur's flesh, but no other marks to speak of. And yet, as the one thing that could harm Freya's favorite son, I supposed it was a fairly creative method of torture. I knew I certainly wouldn't be able to tolerate being tied down and tickled to death by a relative stranger in a grimy Santa Claus outfit in the middle of a horrifying hellscape.

Or, you know, any part of that sentence, really.

"You said you had a message for him?" Loki asked between prods, his voice barely carrying over Baldur's pathetic whimpers.

"From Odin, aye."

Baldur lifted his head to stare at me, a tremendous hope reflected in his eyes, his wretched expression morphing instantly into something smug and far too entitled.

"He said 'tell Baldur that when they're done with him, it will be my turn.'"

Baldur's head flopped back to the table, and he started to cry—in earnest this time, shivering like a distressed poodle.

Loki whistled. "Wowwww...you managed to piss off the Allfather! You. Are. So. Fucked."

Baldur's sobs grew louder.

Loki slapped the god's thigh. "Don't worry, I won't let him have you anytime soon."

"Oy, can we talk outside?" I asked, hoping to get away from the wailing, piteous creature formerly known as Baldur.

"Sure thing." Loki leaned over the god and tapped his nose. "And I'll see *you* in a bit. And try not to ruin the underwear I got you. All I've got left is lady's lingerie."

With that, Loki escorted me out of the shabby little tent they kept Baldur in and together we started walking the perimeter of Loki's camp. I noticed that Fenrir was nowhere to be seen, though I swore I could hear a faint howl on the wind.

"What'd he do, anyway?" I asked, glancing back over my shoulder. "Baldur, I mean."

"To us? Or to end up on Odin's naughty list?"

"Both?"

Loki pursed his lips. "It's a long story. Suffice it to say he won't be hurting anyone else again anytime soon. Besides, didn't you say you had something else you wanted to see me about? Wouldn't you rather talk about that?"

Though it felt like Loki was dodging my question for some reason, I shrugged and began filling him in on the details of my recent trip to Fólkvangr, focusing mainly on my loss of memories and my desire to see them restored. When I was finished, I could tell he'd thought of something from the way he tilted his head.

"What is it?" I asked.

"Well, it's a long shot, but if it's your memory you want to fix, you could always pay the Norns a visit."

"The Norns? Ye mean the weavers who live underground, below Yggdrasil?"

Loki nodded. "Each of them specialize in a particular period of time. Past, present, and future. If you want to know about something that's already happened, then you'll want to talk to Urðr. She's crotchety, but reliable. And not half bad in the sack, if you know what I mean. Back in the day, at least."

I rolled my eyes. "And how would I go about doin' that? Gettin' to Yggdrasil, I mean. Isn't it like a holy place to ye lot?"

Loki buffed his grimy nails on his even grimier coat. "Well, I *could* send you there. For a price."

"What price?"

As if he'd been anticipating this moment since I arrived, Loki produced the bit of mistletoe he'd used to torture Baldur, raised it high into the air between us so that it dangled in the murky half-light, and puckered his lips.

I shoved him. "Not a chance, ye sleaze."

Loki flashed a wicked grin. "Can't blame a god for trying."

"Wanna bet?"

"Tell you what," Loki replied, hoisting a single finger. "I'll send you where you want to go, but only if you promise to take a picture of Fenrir and me before you leave."

"A picture?"

Loki nodded, gravely. "We have to get our Yuletide cards out to friends and family soon, and I'm having a Hel of a time getting us both into frame for a selfie."

"That's it? Ye just want me to take a picture of ye and you'll send me to Yggdrasil?"

"A *good* picture," Loki clarified. "Make sure you take it from my good side, and that you really accentuate my cheekbones. Oh, and mood lighting. We'll need *lots* of mood lighting."

CHAPTER 46

I stepped through my second Gateway in as many hours and was once again left vaguely nauseated by the experience. This time, however, it was not the murky gloom of Niflheim that made it impossible to see, but the brilliant sunlight streaming through the canopy of a tree so enormous that it literally defied comprehension.

As the portal snapped shut behind me and my eyes adjusted to the light, I took a moment to survey my surroundings. The grass beneath my feet was an electric shade of green, the sky a rich, cloudless blue. The temperature was cool but not chilly, the humidity negligible, the wind gentle. In a word: perfect.

At last, I turned my attention to the World Tree for which this place was named, forced to crane my neck towards the heavens in search of the World Tree's uppermost branches, all of which had grown so high they appeared hazy and indistinct—as if they'd reached beyond our atmosphere and out into space.

A sudden wave of vertigo washed over me as I realized just how small—just how insignificant—I was in relation to this improbable monstrosity with its sprawling canopy in the stars and its rambling, realms-deep roots.

Fortunately, whatever existential crisis I was about to suffer was mitigated by the furtive movement of some creature racing along the lower branches.

"Is that a freakin' squirrel?" I said out loud to myself.

The answer was yes.

Of course, calling Ratatoskr—the World Tree's resident Rodentia and Norse mythology's premiere gossip—a squirrel was a lot like saying Fenrir was just a big dog: technically correct, but fundamentally misleading. Much like Fenrir, the difference lay in Ratatoskr's ridiculous size and terrifying aesthetic; he had teeth like shovels and claws that could rend holes in the sides of steel buildings.

He was also, apparently, very fond of decorating.

From every bough for the first thousand feet or so hung some kind of ornament—be it the skull of a troll, a rusted battle axe, a shattered shield, or the tattered feathers of a giant eagle. As I watched, Ratatoskr scuttled across the Yggdrasil's trunk, reached out with one paw, and tied a massive hunk of Bifrosted glass to a particularly sturdy branch where it shone with all the colors of the rainbow.

And then he turned and noticed me.

The lunatic squirrel gave a shrill battle cry and leapt from the tree from hundreds of feet up, all four of his paws extended as if he meant to impale me. I balked and danced backwards, but I needn't have bothered; Ratatoskr landed like a cat some twenty feet ahead before rising up onto his hind legs and pointing with one menacing claw.

"You!"

I pointed at myself. "Me?"

"Yeah, you! Let's flyt."

I stood frozen for a moment, wondering if this demented rodent really meant to attack me. And then I realized he'd said "flyt" and not "fight"—a term referring to a battle of wits popular among sea raiders and Celts. A tradition that involved spitting rhymes back and forth at each other's expense until someone either gave up or the battle became a beef.

So the OG rap battle, basically.

"If you beat me," Ratatoskr continued, "I won't eviscerate you and hang your intestines from my tree. Sound good?"

It did not.

"Why would ye want to eviscerate me in the first place?" I asked, dumbfounded.

"It's my job." The squirrel rubbed his paws together over and over again like a nervous tic.

"Your job is to murder people who come here?"

"If they're unchaperoned, then yes."

I cursed Loki under my breath for sending me here without a warning. And after I'd taken such a good photo of him and his pup, too. Tricky bastard.

I sighed. "Are ye sure we can't just talk t'ings out, instead? I love what you've done with the World Tree, by the way. Very...um, festive."

Ratatoskr's beady little eyes narrowed. "Not that it's any of your business...but I did it to please my Rider. Last time he was here he said his kind enjoy hanging junk on the trees they care for, so I thought he might like it."

"I'm sure he will!" I perked up at the mention of a Rider—another term for Horseman, from what I'd gathered. I cleared my throat and spoke in a sweet, reassuring voice I usually reserved for small children and demented lunatics. "And what's your Rider's name?"

"Why would you need to know that?"

"I was just curious."

"Because you want to copulate with him?"

"What? No! You've got it all—"

"Please, I know how you filthy humans are. Grimm's told me all about the things you do to each other. You're like *animals*."

"I do *not* want to sleep with your Rider!"

"Good. Because I have to warn you, he's already got a mate, and she's scary." Ratatoskr shivered. "You have no idea how scary."

I pretended to study my fingernails while I put the pieces together. A male with a scary mate. A Horseman. Presumably one of Nate's crowd, considering the other Horsemen—the traditional ones —all rode horses.

"Is it Gunnar?" I ventured, reminded of Nate's beefcake of a best friend—a lunarly-challenged confidant who also happened to be married to a badass she-wolf.

"How did you know that? Who told you?!"

"No one told me. I know him."

"Prove it. What's his favorite color?"

"His fav—how should I know?"

"Wrong. It's pink."

"It *is* not!"

"It might be."

"D'ye just ask me what Gunnar's favorite color was when *ye* didn't even know?"

"Maybe. Now, enough idle chit chat. Flyt me right now, or I'm going to make a bracelet out of your spine."

I sighed. "Fine. But if I win, ye have to tell me the fastest way to reach the Norns. That's who I came here to see."

Ratatoskr clapped his paws together. "Deal."

"You'll have to start," I told him. "I've never done this before."

"Don't worry it's easy, just like your mom…"

I started to clench my fists and say something less than cordial before realizing Ratatoskr was waiting for me to finish the line. I tilted my head, considered my reply, and fired back with the first thing I could think of.

"Which makes ye the submissive," I said, "and me mother the dom."

Ratatoskr thumped his tail as if to signal I'd landed a point. "They call me the Nutcracker, because I'm so good with my seed…"

Yuck.

"No they call ye the Nutcracker, because you're so damned crazy."

Another thump. "Hey, you'd better be nice, or else we'll have no choice but to quarrel…"

"Good t'ing I'm not scared of mice, ye sorry excuse for a squirrel."

"Whoa, whoa, whoa…" Ratatoskr's eyes had practically bugged out of his head. "Did you just call me a mouse?"

"Maybe."

For a moment, I swore it looked as though the oversized rodent might launch himself at me, and then he laughed. Or at least I assumed it was a laugh—the chittering sound of his teeth clanking together was something I'd have associated with a jackhammer.

"That was great," he said, his bushy tail swishing across the grass like a massive rake. "Are you sure it was your first—"

Ratatoskr froze, his ears pointing straight up.

"What is it?" I asked, alarmed.

The squirrel turned to face the horizon, where a great big storm cloud had begun to roll in, its interior dancing with red lightning. Feeling a strange sense of ominous dread, I shrank away from it. Ratatoskr, on the other hand, took off towards it like he'd been shot out of a cannon.

"Grimm!" he shouted gleefully as he galloped away. "It's Grimm! My best friend is here!"

"Oy!" I called, my voice carrying despite a sudden gust of wind from that direction. "What about our deal? How do I get to the Norns?"

"Third root on your right, go down, take the second left!" replied Ratatoskr without looking back. "You can't miss it!"

I cursed. "And where are ye goin?!"

But this time he must not have heard me because he never replied.

CHAPTER 47

I followed Ratatoskr's directions as best I could, descending through a gap between a pair of tree roots hidden behind a curtain of hanging vines just as the weather outside took a turn for the worse. Beyond the vines, I discovered a flight of well worn stairs carved from the bedrock that descended into complete and utter darkness. Fortunately, there was a torch mounted into a nearby wall that burst into a cold, silvery flame the instant I wrapped my hand around it.

Using its faint light, I was able to navigate my way down the stairs, ignoring the first several divergent paths in favor of the one Ratstoskr had suggested—a large archway that seemed perpetually steeped in shadow, so much so in fact that my torch dimmed as I passed through.

The chamber beyond led to a living area of sorts, albeit apparently abandoned; the hearth was unlit, the furniture shabby and moth-eaten, and the room unoccupied. Still, I wandered about for a time, thrusting my torch into the darkest of corners and calling out to whomever should have been there. And yet I neither saw nor heard anyone. Indeed, there was a sense of emptiness so pervasive about the place that I could hardly stand it.

And so I moved on, crossing the threshold into another chamber, this one opening up to reveal a much more lavish space, though just as empty. Or at least so it seemed at first glance.

Upon further inspection, I discovered a cup of still steaming tea sitting on the coffee table, the embers of a fire that had been recently put out, and caught the faint whisper of retreating footsteps down a side corridor followed by the tell-tale slamming of a door. In fact, I was just about to go after them when a middle-aged woman appeared in a doorway up ahead.

"You'll have to forgive Skuld, dear," she told me, gesturing to the corridor. "I expect yours is not a future she wishes to see up close. She's become very non-confrontational after all these years. People tend to give her the hardest time, you see."

I opened my mouth, then closed it, and finally jerked a thumb over my shoulder. "The first room was empty, too."

"Urðr's?" the woman said, sounding surprised. "Well, that's odd. I don't suppose you have some horrid past you hoped to rehash, did you?"

"Well, I don't know that I'd call it horrid," I muttered. "But maybe. Kinda."

The woman nodded. "Well then, I imagine Skuld forewarned her, which means she'll have cleared off a while ago. It's the relived trauma, you know. Upsets her stomach. Weak constitution ever since we were girls back in Jötunnheim. But don't worry, I'll be happy to help. Do you like tea? I was making chai."

I hesitated, struck perhaps by the urbanity of this strange woman's—no, this strange giantess', I corrected myself—replies. And yet, she had a very pleasant, no-nonsense quality about her that made it hard to dislike or distrust her.

"Who are you?" I asked.

"Oh that's right. Introductions. My name is Verðandi, although you may know me better as the Norn of Yuletide Present." She winked. "Now come warm yourself by my fire, dear. I don't know what all you've been through, but I can tell you need it."

CHAPTER 48

I sat before a large fire from which heat wafted up in soothing waves, cradling a hot cup of chai tea. The brew had a delightful cinnamon undertone to it and thawed something inside of me that I hadn't realized had frozen. Indeed, for the first time in a long while I felt content to simply sit and relish the moment at hand. And I mean *really* relish it—not that zen, concentrate on your breathing, crap the meditation apps preach.

Eventually, however, I set my empty cup back down on its saucer and turned to the Norn.

"I came here to find out what happened to me over the last six months," I told her. "And I was hopin' your sister would be able to tell me."

"I can see that, yes," Verðandi replied with a gentle smile. "I knew why you came from the moment I laid eyes on you. I also know what you want and don't want. What you think you want and don't want, anyway. What you're thinking about. What you're avoiding thinking about. And yes, I know precisely how uncomfortable that makes you, and I apologize. But that *is* my nature."

I coughed into my fist. "Right. And does any of that mean ye can help me? Maybe ye could convince your sister to see me, now that ye know I'm not here to cause trouble?"

"That I cannot do, I'm afraid. She'll have gone down and locked herself inside her well. Yggdrasil only knows when she'll return. Well, Yggrdrasil and Skuld, I suppose."

"I see." I hung my head. "Another dead end, then, huh?"

"Not necessarily."

"What makes ye say that?"

Verðandi smiled as if to herself. "My gift is not always a gift, you know. It can be difficult, seeing the solution to another's problem in that person's mind and knowing they've yet to realize it, themselves."

"So...why not just tell me?"

"I can't, dear. Without knowing what the future will bring, I dare not risk it. If you are meant to discover the means, I believe you will. If not..." Verðandi shrugged. "Such is fate."

"That's not exactly helpful," I muttered.

"Perhaps not. But I can help you in other ways. You forget, I can see into your mind's eye. I know the questions you want answers to, just as I know that some are in my power to give. Such as the present fate of your friends, the ones whom you worry so very much about."

I bent forward, gripping the arms of the chair I sat in until the wood creaked beneath my hands. "Ye can really do that?"

"Indeed I can. For a price."

"Of course." I settled back in my chair with a sigh. "There's always a price with ye people. What is it?"

"You must tell me a story."

"A story? About what?"

"You, dear. A story from your past. I can only see what *is*, not what was or will be. Stories of the past are, for me especially, a wonderful treat. Oh, but make it a personal story, would you? Something...heartfelt."

The instant the word left the Norn's lips, a memory surfaced. It wasn't a particularly noteworthy memory, so I didn't know why it occurred to me at that moment, only that it did. I was seven or eight at the time, and the snow had blanketed the modest neighborhood park behind my house—coating the ground and filling the slide and piling atop the swings.

I remember I wore a red coat I'd refused to take off all winter long and a pair of yellow boots that clomped when I walked. I should have been wearing gloves and a hat, too, except I'd gotten hot wearing them and had just shoved them into my pockets. Fortunately, Dez, who would have scolded me for doing so, was too busy helping our neighbor and his boy build a snowman to notice.

Indeed, it was the snowman's arms I'd been sent off to collect. I'd found one serviceable branch and was scouring the ground for the other when I noticed a man sitting on a swing. He was tall and dark-haired and handsome enough that I remembered being shy when he smiled at me—even more so when he waved.

"The other stick is over there," he called to me, pointing. "See? That's the one you want."

He was right; the stick he suggested I choose was a near perfect match to the one I already held. I raised both and waved them about, showing off the wicked ninja skills I hoped to one day perfect in my weekly karate class. And the man, seeing this, clapped.

"Very nice," he acknowledged. "Now, shouldn't you be getting back? I'm sure you have someone who cares about you who might be worried if you're gone too long. I know if I had a little girl, I would be."

At the time, I didn't really understand what he was saying. And yet, I took his advice and returned with the sticks. It was only afterwards, however, when I told my Aunt Dez and explained where I'd been, that I realized the threat the man had posed.

"If ye ever see him again, ye come and tell me right away, ye understand? I mean it, Quinn."

Of course, it would be a long time before it occurred to me that the stranger I'd met that day might not have been a stranger at all—and that Dez's fear was not that I'd be abducted, but that I'd be reunited.

With my father.

"Only I never saw him again, so I guess it didn't matter," I finished, hot tears trickling down my cheeks. I swiped them away. "Sorry, I don't know why that made me cry."

"You really don't, do you?" the Norn asked, quietly. Then, as if rousing herself from a stupor, she propped herself up and waved a hand at the fire. "A deal's a deal. Look into the flames, think of those you wish to see, and I shall show you visions of their present moments."

I did as she asked, thinking first of those I'd left behind in Boston and beyond. Within seconds, the flames parted, forming a frame of fire within which I was able to make out all manner of familiar faces.

I saw Max and Robin and Camilla all gathered in front of a television screen playing *Lethal Weapon 2*, the lights of their Christmas tree reflecting off the screen.

I saw Hilde, dressed in a sweater and jeans, hugging her fellow Sickos before stealing a kiss from Leo.

I saw a frowning Othello sitting alone at a table in a crowded restaurant staring at her phone.

I saw Scathach nursing a glass of expensive whiskey while staring out a window at a clear night sky and a gibbous moon.

I saw Christoff in his childrens' room reading a beautifully illustrated copy of *'Twas the Night Before Christmas*.

I saw Cathal curled up in front of a roaring fireplace, his enormous head buried behind his back paw.

I saw a bearded James Hook at the prow of a boat surrounded by ruby red waters, a waifish girl by his side.

I saw a floating island dominating a cloudless sky above a city that belonged to another world.

"Have you seen enough?" the Norn asked.

I blinked as if coming out of a trance, realizing I'd scooted so close to the edge of my seat that I'd risked slipping off and singeing my own eyebrows. I sat back in awe, my mind whirling with the implications of everything I'd just witnessed. And yet, I knew somehow that the gift I'd been given was not meant to be overanalyzed—at least not yet.

"Sorry," I said, shaking my head. "What was that?"

"I asked if you'd seen enough. Or was there someone else you'd like to see?"

I opened my mouth to say no, then closed it. There *was* one person. The man, the wizard, in whose wake I seemed fated to travel. And yet...did I really want to know what Nate Temple was doing at this precise moment? Did I really care, or was I just worried it might end up having something to do with me?

The instant I asked myself that question, however, I knew I had my answer.

"No," I replied, at last. "No, that's everyone."

CHAPTER 49

Verðandi led me to a door, held it open, and passed over my torch. Together, we shared a look of such understanding that I very nearly asked to stay—though I wasn't sure why, or how, our sudden intimacy had come about.

"It's what I know," the Norn explained, no doubt reading my thoughts. "There are few individuals in all the realms who are as easy to like as the person who knows you best and still wishes you well. And I do, child."

I mumbled a thanks.

Verðandi nodded. Then, when I didn't move, she settled a hand on my arm. "Is there something else?"

"I don't know what to do or where to go," I confessed. "I came here to find me lost memories, but it feels like everythin' and everyone is tellin' me to move on."

"Yes, and I can see that you don't want to." Verðandi squeezed my arm. "But life is sometimes unsatisfactory in that way, as you well know."

"Aye. I just feel a little lost, that's all."

"Is that so..." Verðandi trailed off.

"What is it?"

"Nothing, dear. I simply wondered if pointing you in a specific direction would be hurtful or helpful at this juncture."

Now it was my turn to grab her arm. "Please tell me."

The Norn sighed. "Very well. I suggest you leave through this door, but do not go back up the stairs. Go down. Down until the walls are slick with black ice and the air burns your lungs. Then, when you see a doorway made of gold, take a look inside. What you make of what you find there is up to you, as will be the decision you must make."

I nodded adamantly. "T'anks so much, I—"

"A warning, before you leave this place. I may not be able to see the future, but I can guess at it. I know, for instance, that most who come here do so because they are at a crossroads. I can see the paths in front of them without knowing which way they will go. But when I look at you...I see nothing. It is as if you stand on an island. An island you must escape at all costs. I cannot tell you how, only that from now on your choices must be your own."

Though I wasn't entirely sure I understood what she meant or what I was to take from it, I thanked the Norn for the warning, bid her a fond farewell, and left.

Once she shut the door behind me, however, I found myself lingering on the stairwell with her words replaying themselves over and over again in my mind. *Your choices must be your own.* It was good advice.

I fingered the metal ball in my pocket and wondered whether I should give up on this wild turtle dove chase and go home—whatever that meant, these days. I certainly knew I longed to see my friends, especially after looking in on them through the visions in Verðandi's flames. Perhaps everyone was right. Perhaps it would be best if I never learned what had happened, if I simply accepted my losses and moved on.

And yet I descended the stairs, driven by an urge I couldn't put into words. It wasn't mere curiosity, I knew that much. It was something more primal than that. A compulsion, maybe even an obsession.

I simply could *not* leave the stone unturned—not when I knew it was there, and that I could so easily flip it over.

And so I crept down the stairs until my breath plumed and the steps became riddled with hoarfrost, the cold so intense I felt it in the marrow of my bones. Eventually, I came to the doorway Verðandi told me about: rimmed in lustrous gold that had been inscribed with dozens of runes, it led to a cave-like chamber in the middle of which stood a modest well fashioned entirely of cobbled stone.

I crept up to it and found clean water within. I looked around, wondering if perhaps this was Urðr's well. Except her sister had insisted she'd be locked away, and there was no door here to lock. I raised my torch and noticed an inscription on the wall—one I could actually read, as it was repeated from floor to ceiling in multiple languages.

Herein lies Mímisbrunnr, the well of Mimir the Wise.

I turned back to the well in surprise, recalling the tale Alice had spun for me in the tower at Fólkvangr. This was the very well from which Odin drank to gain his prophetic knowledge of the future. On impulse, I crouched down and tried to scoop up some of the water in my cupped hand, but it was like trying to hold air; the liquid sloughed away without leaving even a trace of wetness behind.

I rose, trembling as I recalled the gratuitous details of Alice's story —a tale of willing sacrifice for the sake of knowledge. And it was then, staring down at those still black waters, that I thought to ask myself the question I'd been avoiding until that point: just how far would I be willing to go to discover the truth?

And, more importantly, did I even *really* want to know? If so, then why had I drowned myself in booze at every opportunity? Why had I allowed myself to be pummeled until my face was only so much meat? Why had I avoided pressing the issue with those who claimed to have the answers I so desperately sought?

The answer, I feared, was simple: I was afraid. Afraid of what I'd done. Afraid that I *deserved* all the guilt and shame that rose up, unbidden, at the oddest moments. That whatever I'd done was, somehow, a fate worse than never knowing what happened to my fairy tale armor, my loyal weapon, and even my burgeoning powers.

I was, after all, a flawed person. A bad friend, at times. Hot tempered. Immature. Cruel. I had almost as much difficulty expressing love as I did receiving it. Which was to say nothing of how self-destructive I could be.

Perhaps I had done something truly terrible. Something genuinely irredeemable. What then?

Though to be fair, I reminded myself forcefully, I had my finer traits, as well. I was fiercely loyal and extremely protective of those I cared about. I was a hard worker. I could be clever when the situation called for it. I was courageous, especially under pressure. Hell, I'd stared death in the face so many times even his chosen representative couldn't scare me.

And, perhaps most noteworthy of all, I'd always been the sort of person to take my licks without flinching.

Which was how I knew I could do this.

No.

That I *had* to do this.

Because if I didn't, it meant I was a coward—a word I would rather die than be associated with.

And so, without warning or hesitation, I drove three of my own fingers into the socket of my right eye.

The pain was both immediate and unbelievably nauseating, and yet I managed to wrench back and forth until the connective tissue tore and I was at last able to fling the offending organ towards the well in a spray of blood and viscera. It landed with a soft plop and bobbed there, suspended for just a moment, before finally submerging.

I, of course, was in far too much agony to relish this. In fact, I didn't even realize I'd collapsed to my knees until my voice broke and the screams stopped echoing back at me.

It was then, as I clutched at my own face and fought back a sob, that I noticed the chalice. It dipped into the well and then floated in the air towards me as if carried by an invisible hand, bathed in the same infernal fire that burned cold from my forgotten torch. Once within reach, I clasped both hands around it and, with the desperation of a woman dying of thirst, tossed back its bitter contents.

When at last I managed to look up again, warm blood had gushed all down my face, mingling with a trail of hot tears.

I'd have liked to claim those tears were the result of pain; they weren't. They were tears of grief. Tears of horror and of loss. For—from the very moment I tasted the pitch black waters of Mimir's Well —I knew precisely what I had done...and why I'd worked so hard to suppress it.

Indeed, I remembered *everything*.

∿

Quinn MacKenna will return...

∿

∿

Turn the page to read a sample of **<u>OBSIDIAN SON</u>** *- Nate Temple Book 1 - or* **BUY ONLINE (It's FREE with a Kindle Unlimited subscription).** *Nate Temple is a billionaire wizard from St. Louis. He rides a bloodthirsty unicorn and drinks with the Four Horsemen. He even cow-tipped the Minotaur. Once...*

TRY: OBSIDIAN SON (NATE TEMPLE #1)

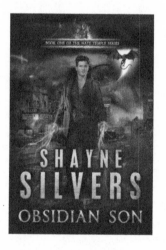

There was no room for emotion in a hate crime. I had to be cold. Heartless. This was just another victim. Nothing more. No face, no name.

Frosted blades of grass crunched under my feet, sounding to my ears like the symbolic glass that one would shatter under a napkin at a Jewish wedding. The noise would have threatened to give away my stealthy advance as I stalked through the moonlit field, but I was no novice and had planned accordingly. Being a wizard, I was able to muffle all sensory evidence with a fine cloud of magic—no sounds, and no smells. Nifty. But if I made the spell much stronger, the anomaly would be too obvious to my prey.

I knew the consequences for my dark deed tonight. If caught, jail time or possibly even a gruesome, painful death. But if I succeeded, the look of fear and surprise in my victim's eyes before his world collapsed around him, it was well worth the risk. I simply couldn't help myself; I had to take him down.

I knew the cops had been keeping tabs on my car, but I was confident that they hadn't followed me. I hadn't seen a tail on my way here but seeing as how they frowned on this kind of thing, I had taken a circuitous route just in case. I was safe. I hoped.

Then my phone chirped at me as I received a text.

I practically jumped out of my skin, hissing instinctively. "Motherf —" I cut off abruptly, remembering the whole stealth aspect of my mission. I was off to a stellar start. I had forgotten to silence the damned phone. *Stupid, stupid, stupid!*

My heart felt like it was on the verge of exploding inside my chest with such thunderous violence that I briefly envisioned a mystifying Rorschach blood-blot that would have made coroners and psychologists drool.

My body remained tense as I swept my gaze over the field, fearing that I had been made. Precious seconds ticked by without any change in my surroundings, and my breathing finally began to slow as my pulse returned to normal. Hopefully, my magic had muted the phone and my resulting outburst. I glanced down at the phone to scan the text and then typed back a quick and angry response before I switched the cursed device to vibrate.

Now, where were we?

I continued on, the lining of my coat constricting my breathing. Or maybe it was because I was leaning forward in anticipation. *Breathe*, I chided myself. *He doesn't know you're here.* All this risk for a book. It had better be worth it.

I'm taller than most, and not abnormally handsome, but I knew how to play the genetic cards I had been dealt. I had shaggy, dirty blonde hair—leaning more towards brown with each passing year—and my frame was thick with well-earned muscle, yet I was still lean. I had once been told that my eyes were like twin emeralds pitted against the golden-brown tufts of my hair—a face like a jewelry box. Of course, that was two bottles of wine into a date, so I could have been a little foggy on her quote. Still, I liked to imagine that was how everyone saw me.

But tonight, all that was masked by magic.

I grinned broadly as the outline of the hairy hulk finally came into view. He was blessedly alone—no nearby sentries to give me away. That was always a risk when performing this ancient rite-of-passage. I tried to keep the grin on my face from dissolving into a maniacal cackle.

My skin danced with energy, both natural and unnatural, as I manipulated the threads of magic floating all around me. My victim stood just ahead, oblivious to the world of hurt that I was about to unleash. Even with his millennia of experience, he didn't stand a chance. I had done this so many times that the routine of it was my only enemy. I lost count of how many times I had been told not to do it again; those who knew declared it *cruel, evil, and sadistic*. But what fun wasn't? Regardless, that wasn't enough to stop me from doing it again. And again. And again.

It was an addiction.

The pungent smell of manure filled the air, latching onto my nostril hairs. I took another step, trying to calm my racing pulse. A glint of gold reflected in the silver moonlight, but my victim remained motionless, hopefully unaware or all was lost. I wouldn't make it out alive if he knew I was here. Timing was everything.

I carefully took the last two steps, a lifetime between each, watching the legendary monster's ears, anxious and terrified that I would catch even so much as a twitch in my direction. Seeing nothing, a fierce grin split my unshaven cheeks. My spell had worked! I raised my palms an inch away from their target, firmly planted my feet, and squared my shoulders. I took one silent, calming breath, and then heaved forward with every ounce of physical strength I could muster. As well as a teensy-weensy boost of magic. Enough to goose him good.

"*MOOO!!!*" The sound tore through the cool October night like an unstoppable freight train. *Thud-splat!* The beast collapsed sideways onto the frosted grass; straight into a steaming patty of cow shit, cow dung, or, if you really wanted to church it up, a Meadow Muffin. But to me, shit is, and always will be, shit.

Cow tipping. It doesn't get any better than that in Missouri.

Especially when you're tipping the *Minotaur*. Capital M. I'd tipped plenty of ordinary cows before, but never the legendary variety.

Razor-blade hooves tore at the frozen earth as the beast struggled to stand, his grunts of rage vibrating the air. I raised my arms triumphantly. "Boo-yah! Temple 1, Minotaur 0!" I crowed. Then I very bravely prepared to protect myself. Some people just couldn't take a joke. *Cruel, evil,* and *sadistic* cow tipping may be, but by hell, it was a *rush*. The legendary beast turned his gaze on me after gaining his feet, eyes ablaze as his body...*shifted* from his bull disguise into his notorious, well-known bipedal form. He unfolded to his full height on two tree trunk-thick legs, his hooves having magically trans-formed into heavily booted feet. The thick, gold ring dangling from his snotty snout quivered as the Minotaur panted, and his dense, corded muscles contracted over his now human-like chest. As I stared up into those brown eyes, I actually felt sorry...for, well, myself.

"I have killed greater men than you for lesser offense," he growled.

His voice sounded like an angry James Earl Jones—like Mufasa talking to Scar.

"You have shit on your shoulder, Asterion." I ignited a roiling ball of fire in my palm in order to see his eyes more clearly. By no means was it a defensive gesture on my part. It was just dark. Under the weight of his glare, I somehow managed to keep my face composed, even though my fraudulent, self-denial had curled up into the fetal position and started whimpering. I hoped using a form of his ancient name would give me brownie points. Or maybe just not-worthy-of-killing points.

The beast grunted, eyes tightening, and I sensed the barest hesitation. "Nate Temple...your name would look splendid on my already long list of slain idiots." Asterion took a threatening step forward, and I thrust out my palm in warning, my roiling flame blue now.

"You lost fair and square, Asterion. Yield or perish." The beast's shoulders sagged slightly. Then he finally nodded to himself in resignation, appraising me with the scrutiny of a worthy adversary. "Your time comes, Temple, but I will grant you this. You've got a pair of stones on you to rival Hercules."

I reflexively glanced in the direction of the myth's own crown jewels before jerking my gaze away. Some things you simply couldn't un-see. "Well, I won't be needing a wheelbarrow any time soon, but overcompensating today keeps future lower-back pain away."

The Minotaur blinked once, and then he bellowed out a deep, contagious, snorting laughter. Realizing I wasn't about to become a murder statistic, I couldn't help but join in. It felt good. It had been a while since I had allowed myself to experience genuine laughter.

In the harsh moonlight, his bulk was even more intimidating as he towered head and shoulders above me. This was the beast that had fed upon human sacrifices for countless years while imprisoned in Daedalus' Labyrinth in Greece. And all that protein had not gone to waste, forming a heavily woven musculature over the beast's body that made even Mr. Olympia look puny.

From the neck up, he was now entirely bull, but the rest of his body more closely resembled a thickly furred man. But, as shown moments ago, he could adapt his form to his environment, never appearing fully human, but able to make his entire form appear as a bull when necessary. For instance, how he had looked just before I tipped him. Maybe he had been scouting the field for heifers before I had so efficiently killed the mood.

His bull face was also covered in thick, coarse hair—he even sported a long, wavy beard of sorts, and his eyes were the deepest brown I had ever seen. Cow-shit brown. His snout jutted out, emphasizing the golden ring dangling from his glistening nostrils, and both glinted in the luminous glow of the moon. The metal was at least an inch thick and etched with runes of a language long forgotten. Wide, aged ivory horns sprouted from each temple, long enough to skewer a wizard with little effort. He was nude except for a massive beaded necklace and a pair of worn leather boots that were big enough to stomp a size twenty-five imprint in my face if he felt so inclined.

I hoped our blossoming friendship wouldn't end that way. I really did.

Because friends didn't let friends wear boots naked...

~

Get your copy of OBSIDIAN SON online today! http://www.shayne-silvers.com/l/38474

~

If you enjoyed the BLADE or UNDERWORLD movies, turn the page to read a sample of DEVIL'S DREAM—the first book in the new SHADE OF DEVIL series by Shayne Silvers.
Or get the book ONLINE! http://www.shaynesilvers.com/l/738833

Before the now-infamous Count Dracula ever tasted his first drop of blood, Sorin Ambrogio owned the night. Humanity fearfully called him the Devil...

TRY: DEVIL'S DREAM (SHADE OF DEVIL #1)

God damned me.

He—in his infinite, omnipotent wisdom—declared for all to hear...

Let there be pain...

In the exact center of this poor bastard's soul.

And that merciless smiting woke me from a dead sleep and thrust me into a body devoid of every sensation but blinding agony.

I tried to scream but my throat felt as dry as dust, only permitting me to emit a rasping, whistling hiss that brought on yet *more* pain. My skin burned and throbbed while my bones creaked and groaned with each full-body tremor. My claws sunk into a hard surface beneath me and I was distantly surprised they hadn't simply shattered upon contact.

My memory was an immolated ruin—each fragment of thought merely an elusive fleck of ash or ember that danced through my fog of despair as I struggled to catch one and hold onto it long enough to recall what had brought me to this bleak existence. How I had become this poor, wretched, shell of a man. I couldn't even remember my own *name*; it was all I could do to simply survive this profound horror.

After what seemed an eternity, the initial pain began to slowly ebb, but I quickly realized that it had only triggered a cascade of smaller, more numerous tortures—like ripples caused by a boulder thrown into a pond.

I couldn't find the strength to even attempt to open my crusted eyes, and my abdomen was a solid knot of gnawing hunger so overwhelming that I felt like I was being pulled down into the earth by a lead weight. My fingers tingled and burned so fiercely that I wondered if the skin had been peeled away while I slept. Since they were twitching involuntarily, at least I knew that the muscles and tendons were still attached.

I held onto that sliver of joy, that beacon of hope.

I stubbornly gritted my teeth, but even that slight movement made the skin over my face stretch tight enough to almost tear. I willed myself to relax as I tried to process *why* I was in so much pain, where I was, how I had gotten here, and...*who* I even was? A singular thought finally struck me like an echo of the faintest of whispers, giving me something to latch onto.

Hunger.

I let out a crackling gasp of relief at finally grasping an independent answer of some kind, but I was unable to draw enough moisture onto my tongue to properly swallow. Understanding that I was hungry had seemed to alleviate a fraction of my pain. The answer to at least one question distracted me long enough to allow me to think. And despite my hunger, I felt something tantalizingly delicious slowly coursing down my throat, desperately attempting to alleviate my starvation.

Even though my memory was still enshrouded in fog, I was entirely certain that it was incredibly dangerous for me to feel this hungry. This...*thirsty*. Dangerous for both myself and anyone nearby. I tried to remember why it was so dangerous but the reason eluded me. Instead, an answer to a different question emerged from my mind like a specter from the mist—and I felt myself begin to smile as a modicum of strength slowly took root deep within me.

"Sorin..." I croaked. My voice echoed, letting me know that I was in an enclosed space of some kind. "My name is Sorin Ambrogio. And I need..." I trailed off uncertainly, unable to finish my own thought.

"Blood," a man's deep voice answered from only a few paces away. "You need more blood."

I hissed instinctively, snapping my eyes open for the first time since waking. I had completely forgotten to check my surroundings, too consumed with my own pain to bother with my other senses. I had been asleep so long that even the air seemed to burn my eyes like smoke, forcing me to blink rapidly. No, the air *was* filled with pungent, aromatic smoke, but not like the smoke from the fires in my—

I shuddered involuntarily, blocking out the thought for some unknown reason.

Beneath the pungent smoke, the air was musty and damp. Through it all, I smelled the delicious, coppery scent of hot, powerful blood.

I had been resting atop a raised stone plinth—almost like a table —in a depthless, shadowy cavern. I appreciated the darkness because any light would have likely blinded me in my current state. I couldn't see the man who had spoken, but the area was filled with silhouettes of what appeared to be tables, crates, and other shapes that could easily conceal him. I focused on my hearing and almost instantly noticed a seductively familiar, *beating* sound.

A noise as delightful as a child's first belly-laugh…

A beautiful woman's sigh as she locked eyes with you for the first time.

The gentle crackling of a fireplace on a brisk, snowy night.

Thump-thump.

Thump-thump.

Thump-thump.

The sound became *everything* and my vision slowly began to sharpen, the room brightening into shades of gray. My pain didn't disappear, but it was swiftly muted as I tracked the sound.

I inhaled deeply, my eyes riveting on a far wall as my nostrils flared, pinpointing the source of the savory perfume and the seductive beating sound. I didn't recall sitting up, but I realized that I was suddenly leaning forward and that the room was continuing to brighten into paler shades of gray, burning away the last of the remaining shadows—despite the fact that there was no actual light. And it grew clearer as I focused on the seductive sound.

Until I finally spotted a man leaning against the far wall. *Thump-thump. Thump-thump. Thump-thump…* I licked my lips ravenously, setting my hands on the cool stone table as I prepared to set my feet on the ground.

Food…

The man calmly lifted his hand and a sharp *clicking* sound suddenly echoed from the walls. The room abruptly flooded with light so bright and unexpected that it felt like my eyes had exploded. Worse, what seemed like a trio of radiant stars was not more than a span from my face —so close that I could feel the direct heat from their flare. I recoiled with a snarl, momentarily forgetting all about food as I shielded my eyes with a hand and prepared to defend myself. I leaned away from the bright lights, wondering why I couldn't smell smoke from the flickering flames. I squinted, watching the man's feet for any indication of movement.

Half a minute went by as my vision slowly began to adjust, and the man didn't even shift his weight—almost as if he was granting me time enough to grow accustomed to the sudden light. Which...didn't make any sense. Hadn't it been an attack? I hesitantly lowered my hand from my face, reassessing the situation and my surroundings.

I stared in wonder as I realized that the orbs were not made of flame, but rather what seemed to be pure light affixed to polished metal stands. Looking directly at them hurt, so I studied them side-long, making sure to also keep the man in my peripheral vision. He had to be a sorcerer of some kind. Who else could wield pure light without fire?

"Easy, Sorin," the man murmured in a calming baritone. "I can't see as well as you in the dark, but it looked like you were about to do something unnecessarily stupid. Let me turn them down a little."

He didn't wait for my reply, but the room slowly dimmed after another clicking sound.

I tried to get a better look at the stranger—wondering where he had come from, where he had taken me, and who he was. One thing was obvious—he knew magic. "Where did you learn this sorcery?" I rasped, gesturing at the orbs of light.

"Um. Hobby Lobby."

"I've never heard of him," I hissed, coughing as a result of my parched throat.

"I'm not even remotely surprised by that," he said dryly. He extended his other hand and I gasped to see an impossibility—a transparent bag as clear as new glass. And it was *flexible*, swinging back and forth like a bulging coin purse or a clear water-skin. My momentary wonder at the magical material evaporated as I recognized the crimson liquid *inside* the bag.

Blood.

He lobbed it at me underhanded without a word of warning. I hissed as I desperately—and with exceeding caution—caught it from the air lest it fall and break open. I gasped as the clear bag of blood settled into my palms and, before I consciously realized it, I tore off the corner with my fangs, pressed it to my lips, and squeezed the bag in one explosive, violent gesture. The ruby fluid gushed into my mouth and over my face, dousing my almost forgotten pain as swiftly as a bucket of water thrown on hot coals.

I felt my eyes roll back into my skull and my body shuddered as I lost my balance and fell from the stone table. I landed on my back but I was too overwhelmed to care as I stretched out my arms and legs. I groaned in rapture, licking at my lips like a wild animal. The ruby nectar was a living serpent of molten oil as it slithered down into my stomach, nurturing and healing me almost instantly. It was the most wonderful sensation I could imagine—almost enough to make me weep.

Like a desert rain, my parched tongue and throat absorbed the blood so quickly and completely that I couldn't even savor the heady flavor. This wasn't a joyful feast; this was survival, a necessity. My body guzzled it, instantly using the liquid to repair the damage, pain, and the cloud of fog that had enshrouded me.

I realized that I was laughing. The sound echoed into the vast stone space like rolling thunder.

Because I had remembered something else.

The world's First Vampire was *back*.

And he was still *very* hungry.

~

Get the full book ONLINE! http://www.shaynesilvers.com/l/738833

Check out Shayne's other books. He's written a few without Cameron helping him. Some of them are marginally decent—easily a 4 out of 10.

MAKE A DIFFERENCE

Reviews are the most powerful tools in our arsenal when it comes to getting attention for our books. Much as we'd like to, we don't have the financial muscle of a New York publisher.

But we do have something much more powerful and effective than that, and it's something that those publishers would kill to get their hands on.

A committed and loyal bunch of readers.

Honest reviews of our books help bring them to the attention of other readers.

If you've enjoyed this book, we would be very grateful if you could spend just five minutes leaving a review on our book's Amazon page.

Thank you very much in advance.

ACKNOWLEDGMENTS

From Cameron:

I'd like to thank Shayne, for paving the way in style. Kori, for an introduction that would change my life. My three wonderful sisters, for showing me what a strong, independent woman looks and sounds like. And, above all, my parents, for—literally—everything.

From Shayne (the self-proclaimed prettiest one):

Team Temple and the Den of Freaks on Facebook have become family to me. I couldn't do it without die-hard readers like them.

I would also like to thank you, the reader. I hope you enjoyed reading *YULETIDE PUNCH* as much as we enjoyed writing it. Be sure to check out the two crossover series in the TempleVerse: **The Nate Temple Series** and the **Feathers and Fire Series**.

And last, but definitely not least, I thank my wife, Lexy. Without your support, none of this would have been possible.

ABOUT CAMERON O'CONNELL

Cameron O'Connell is a Jack-of-All-Trades and Master of Some.

He writes The Phantom Queen Diaries, a series in The Temple-Verse, about Quinn MacKenna, a mouthy black magic arms dealer trading favors in Boston. All she wants? A round-trip ticket to the Fae realm...and maybe a drink on the house.

A former member of the United States military, a professional model, and English teacher, Cameron finds time to write in the mornings after his first cup of coffee...and in the evenings after his thirty-seventh. Follow him, and the TempleVerse founder, Shayne Silvers, online for all sorts of insider tips, giveaways, and new release updates!

Get Down with Cameron Online

facebook.com/Cameron-OConnell-788806397985289

amazon.com/author/cameronoconnell

bookbub.com/authors/cameron-o-connell

twitter.com/thecamoconnell

instagram.com/camoconnellauthor

goodreads.com/cameronoconnell

ABOUT SHAYNE SILVERS

Shayne is a man of mystery and power, whose power is exceeded only by his mystery...

He currently writes the Amazon Bestselling **Nate Temple** Series, which features a foul-mouthed wizard from St. Louis. He rides a bloodthirsty unicorn, drinks with Achilles, and is pals with the Four Horsemen.

He also writes the Amazon Bestselling **Feathers and Fire** Series —a second series in the TempleVerse. The story follows a rookie spell-slinger named Callie Penrose who works for the Vatican in Kansas City. Her problem? Hell seems to know more about her past than she does.

He coauthors **The Phantom Queen Diaries**—a third series set in The TempleVerse—with Cameron O'Connell. The story follows Quinn MacKenna, a mouthy black magic arms dealer in Boston. All she wants? A round-trip ticket to the Fae realm...and maybe a drink on the house.

He also writes the **Shade of Devil Series**, which tells the story of Sorin Ambrogio—the world's FIRST vampire. He was put into a magical slumber by a Native American Medicine Man when the Americas were first discovered by Europeans. Sorin wakes up after five-hundred years to learn that his protégé, Dracula, stole his reputation and that no one has ever even heard of Sorin Ambrogio. The streets of New York City will run with blood as Sorin reclaims his legend.

Shayne holds two high-ranking black belts, and can be found writing in a coffee shop, cackling madly into his computer screen while pounding shots of espresso. He's hard at work on the newest books in the TempleVerse—You can find updates on new releases or chronological reading order on the next page, his website, or any of his social media accounts. **Follow him online for all sorts of groovy goodies, giveaways, and new release updates:**

Get Down with Shayne Online
www.shaynesilvers.com
info@shaynesilvers.com

facebook.com/shaynesilversfanpage
amazon.com/author/shaynesilvers
bookbub.com/profile/shayne-silvers
instagram.com/shaynesilversofficial
twitter.com/shaynesilvers
goodreads.com/ShayneSilvers

BOOKS BY THE AUTHORS

CHRONOLOGY: All stories in the TempleVerse are shown in chronological order on the following page

PHANTOM QUEEN DIARIES

(Set in the TempleVerse)

by Cameron O'Connell & Shayne Silvers

COLLINS (Prequel novella #0 in the 'LAST CALL' anthology)

WHISKEY GINGER

COSMOPOLITAN

MOTHERLUCKER (Novella #2.5 in the 'LAST CALL' anthology)

OLD FASHIONED

DARK AND STORMY

MOSCOW MULE

WITCHES BREW

SALTY DOG

SEA BREEZE

HURRICANE

BRIMSTONE KISS

MOONSHINE

YULETIDE PUNCH

NATE TEMPLE SERIES

(Main series in the TempleVerse)

by Shayne Silvers

FAIRY TALE - FREE prequel novella #0 for my subscribers

OBSIDIAN SON

BLOOD DEBTS

GRIMM

SILVER TONGUE

BEAST MASTER

BEERLYMPIAN (Novella #5.5 in the 'LAST CALL' anthology)

TINY GODS

DADDY DUTY (Novella #6.5)

WILD SIDE

WAR HAMMER

NINE SOULS

HORSEMAN

LEGEND

KNIGHTMARE

ASCENSION

CARNAGE

SAVAGE

FEATHERS AND FIRE SERIES

(Also set in the TempleVerse)

by Shayne Silvers

UNCHAINED

RAGE

WHISPERS

ANGEL'S ROAR

MOTHERLUCKER (Novella #4.5 in the 'LAST CALL' anthology)

SINNER

BLACK SHEEP

GODLESS

ANGHELLIC

TRINITY

HALO BREAKER

ANGEL DUST

CHRONOLOGICAL ORDER: TEMPLEVERSE

FAIRY TALE (TEMPLE PREQUEL)

OBSIDIAN SON (TEMPLE 1)

BLOOD DEBTS (TEMPLE 2)

GRIMM (TEMPLE 3)

SILVER TONGUE (TEMPLE 4)

BEAST MASTER (TEMPLE 5)

BEERLYMPIAN (TEMPLE 5.5)

TINY GODS (TEMPLE 6)

DADDY DUTY (TEMPLE NOVELLA 6.5)

UNCHAINED (FEATHERS...1)

RAGE (FEATHERS...2)

WILD SIDE (TEMPLE 7)

WAR HAMMER (TEMPLE 8)

WHISPERS (FEATHERS...3)

COLLINS (PHANTOM 0)

WHISKEY GINGER (PHANTOM...1)

NINE SOULS (TEMPLE 9)

COSMOPOLITAN (PHANTOM...2)

ANGEL'S ROAR (FEATHERS...4)

MOTHERLUCKER (FEATHERS 4.5, PHANTOM 2.5)

SHADE OF DEVIL SERIES

(Not part of the TempleVerse)

by Shayne Silvers

DEVIL'S DREAM

DEVIL'S CRY

DEVIL'S BLOOD

DEVIL'S DUE (*coming 2022...*)

Made in the USA
Coppell, TX
29 December 2021

70370701R20135